ROBERTA GLACKEN

Snowed Inn

1

Chapter 1

The snow was relentless. It fell in thick, blinding sheets, erasing everything beyond the edge of the road. Clara Evans tightened her grip on the steering wheel, knuckles white, eyes narrowed against the storm. The tires of her SUV struggled for traction, slipping every now and then on the icy surface. She'd underestimated the storm, and now, the mountain road felt like it was stretching endlessly ahead of her, leading her deeper into the heart of the wilderness.

The GPS flickered, lost its signal, and finally went dark. Clara cursed under her breath. Not like she had much choice now. She was too far in to turn back, and according to the directions she'd memorized before losing signal, the inn should be close. Very close. She hoped.

A gust of wind rattled the car, pushing it sideways on the narrow road. Clara clenched her jaw, focused on the faint outline of the road ahead. Just a bit further. She repeated the thought like a mantra, trying to ignore the way her heart was pounding in her chest. It was just a storm. People drove in storms all the time.

Except not this storm, not this road.

The SUV's headlights finally picked up something in the distance—a dark shape, standing out against the white. Clara exhaled, a shaky breath she hadn't realized she'd been holding. The inn. It had to be the inn.

Snowridge Inn was an imposing structure, even from a distance. The building seemed to rise up out of the snow, its steep rooflines and tall chimneys disappearing into the swirling white. As she pulled into the small, snow-covered parking area, Clara could see warm light glowing from the windows, a beacon of hope in the otherwise bleak landscape.

She parked, turned off the engine, and for a moment, just sat there, listening to the ticking of the cooling engine and the muffled roar of the wind outside. It was so quiet, so isolated. The city, with its noise and its chaos, felt a million miles away.

"Just get inside," she whispered to herself, forcing her hands to unclench from the steering wheel. She grabbed her bag from the passenger seat and opened the door, bracing herself against the icy blast of wind that rushed in.

The cold hit her like a wall. Clara hunched her shoulders, pulling her coat tighter around her as she trudged through the snow toward the entrance. The wind whipped her hair into her face, stinging her eyes with icy flakes. She could barely see the path, already half-covered in fresh snow, but the light from the inn guided her, pulling her forward.

The front door opened just as she reached it, and a woman stepped out into the wind. "You must be Clara!" she called over the storm, her voice warm and welcoming despite the harsh weather. She had to be the innkeeper, Margaret Whitaker. Clara had spoken to her on the phone when she made the reservation.

"Yeah, that's me," Clara replied, her voice muffled by the scarf wrapped around her face. She hurried up the steps and into the shelter of the porch.

"Come on in," Margaret said, holding the door wide. "You must be freezing."

The warmth hit Clara as soon as she stepped inside, wrapping around her like a comforting embrace. The interior of the inn was exactly what she'd hoped for—wood-paneled walls, a large stone fireplace crackling with a roaring fire, and Christmas decorations that added a festive, cozy touch to the rustic charm of the place.

Margaret shut the door behind her, shutting out the storm. "Let me take your coat," she offered, already reaching to help Clara out of her snow-dusted outerwear.

"Thanks," Clara said, unwinding the scarf from her face and handing it, along with her coat, to Margaret. "That storm came out of nowhere."

"Typical for these mountains," Margaret replied, shaking out the coat before hanging it on a nearby rack. "One minute, it's just a flurry, and the next, you're in the middle of a blizzard."

Clara smiled, though she still felt a bit shaky from the drive. "I thought I wasn't going to make it for a minute there."

"But you did," Margaret said with a reassuring smile. "And you're safe now. How was the drive up?"

"Long. And stressful," Clara admitted, rubbing her cold hands together. "But this place—" She glanced around the lobby, taking in the warm glow of the lights, the inviting furniture arranged around the fireplace. "This is exactly what I needed."

"I'm glad to hear that," Margaret said, genuine warmth in her voice. "We've got a small group here for the holidays. Just a few other guests. Everyone's gathered in the lounge right now, warming up by the fire. Why don't you join them? I'll bring your bags up to your room."

"Are you sure? I can—"

"Don't worry about it," Margaret insisted. "You look like you could use a glass of wine and some relaxation. I'll take care of everything."

Clara hesitated for a moment, then nodded. "Thank you, Margaret. I really appreciate it."

"Not at all," Margaret replied with a smile. "Go on, the lounge is just through there."

Clara followed the direction Margaret indicated, walking down a short hallway that opened up into a large, inviting room. The fire in the lounge was even bigger than the one in the lobby, its flames casting a warm, flickering light over the room. Several plush armchairs and sofas were arranged around the hearth, and a small group of people were seated there, talking quietly. The atmosphere was cozy, intimate, the kind of place where you could easily lose track of time.

She hovered in the doorway for a moment, unsure whether to interrupt. One of the guests, a man in his sixties with a kind face and a thick woolen sweater, noticed her and smiled.

"Come on in," he said, gesturing to an empty seat near the fire. "You must be Clara. Margaret mentioned you were coming."

Clara smiled back, feeling a little more at ease. "That's right. I'm Clara Evans. I hope I'm not interrupting."

"Not at all," the man replied. "I'm Charles Anderson. And this is Emma, Sarah, and Daniel." He pointed to each of the other guests in turn.

Emma, a woman around Clara's age with short brown hair and an anxious energy about her, gave a small wave. "Hi."

"Hi," Clara replied, noting the way Emma's eyes flitted around the room, never settling on one thing for too long.

Sarah and Daniel, the couple sitting together on a nearby sofa, nodded in greeting. Sarah was strikingly beautiful, with dark hair and sharp features, while Daniel had the look of someone who was used to getting his way. They both had an air of detached politeness, as if they were here out of obligation rather than desire.

"Nice to meet you all," Clara said, taking the seat Charles had offered. The fire was warm, almost too warm after the bitter cold outside, but Clara welcomed the heat, letting it chase away the lingering chill in her bones.

"Margaret mentioned you're here to get away from the city," Charles said, his tone friendly and curious.

Clara nodded, not surprised that Margaret had shared that detail. "Yeah, just needed a break from everything."

"I know the feeling," Charles replied with a knowing smile. "There's something about this place, isn't there? It's like stepping back in time, away from all the noise and distractions."

"That's exactly what I was looking for," Clara admitted, her shoulders relaxing for the first time in what felt like weeks. "It's been a rough few months."

Emma glanced at her, curiosity piqued. "What do you do? For work, I mean."

"I'm a journalist," Clara said, a hint of weariness creeping into her voice. "Or I was, anyway. I guess I still am, just… in transition."

"Transition?" Charles echoed, raising an eyebrow.

Clara hesitated, not really wanting to get into the details. "I lost my job. Things didn't exactly go as planned."

Charles nodded, his expression sympathetic. "Sorry to hear

that. But sometimes a change of scenery is exactly what you need. I've been coming to this inn for years, and every time I leave, I feel a little more… centered, I suppose."

"That's what I'm hoping for," Clara said, appreciating his kindness. "Just some time to figure things out."

"Well, you've come to the right place," Charles said, leaning back in his chair. "Snowridge Inn has a way of making the world seem a little less overwhelming."

Clara allowed herself to relax further, sinking into the comfortable chair. The fire crackled softly, and for a moment, she simply enjoyed the warmth, the quiet murmur of conversation around her, and the soft glow of the Christmas lights. This was what she had wanted—peace, a chance to breathe, to escape from the noise of her life. And yet, despite the comfort, there was a small, nagging feeling in the back of her mind, something she couldn't quite put her finger on.

She shook it off. This was what she needed. A place to clear her head, nothing more. The storm outside, the isolation, it was all part of the charm. She was safe here, away from everything that had been weighing her down.

Margaret appeared in the doorway, carrying a tray with a bottle of wine and several glasses. "I thought you all might like a little something to warm up," she said with a smile, setting the tray down on a small table by the fire.

"Perfect timing," Charles said, reaching for a glass. "This is exactly what we need."

Margaret poured the wine, handing a glass to each of them. Clara accepted hers with a grateful smile. "Thank you, Margaret. For everything."

"Of course," Margaret replied warmly. "That's what we're here for. To make sure you all have a peaceful, relaxing stay."

As Margaret moved around the room, chatting briefly with each of the guests, Clara found herself watching the other woman closely. There was something about Margaret—something calming, reassuring. The way she moved, the way she spoke, it was clear she cared deeply about this inn and its guests. But there was also something else, something just beneath the surface that Clara couldn't quite pin down.

Margaret caught her gaze and smiled. "Everything all right, Clara?"

Clara blinked, realizing she'd been staring. "Oh, yes, sorry. Just… thinking."

"About anything in particular?" Margaret asked, her tone light but curious.

Clara hesitated, then shook her head. "Just appreciating how peaceful it is here. It's exactly what I needed."

Margaret nodded, satisfied with the answer. "I'm glad to hear that. If you need anything, don't hesitate to ask. We're here to make sure your stay is as comfortable as possible."

As Margaret left the room, Clara sipped her wine, trying to shake off the strange feeling that had settled over her. It was just the storm, she told herself. The isolation, the quiet. It was different from what she was used to, that was all. It would take a little time to adjust.

The conversation in the room picked up again, the other guests exchanging stories about their lives, their work, their reasons for coming to Snowridge Inn. Clara listened, but didn't contribute much, content to observe. Charles seemed to be the most at ease, talking freely about his years of visiting the inn, the peace he found here. Emma, on the other hand, was more reserved, her responses short and to the point, as if she were holding something back.

Sarah and Daniel were harder to read. They spoke occasionally, but mostly to each other, their words quiet, almost secretive. There was a tension between them, something unspoken that hung in the air like a heavy cloud.

"Is this your first time here?" Clara asked, directing the question to the couple.

Daniel looked at her, his expression guarded. "Yeah, first time. Thought it would be a nice getaway for the holidays."

"And how are you finding it so far?" Clara pressed, trying to gauge their mood.

"It's… nice," Sarah replied, her tone polite but distant. "Very quiet."

"Quiet is good," Charles chimed in, as if trying to lighten the mood. "Especially in this day and age. Sometimes you need a place where you can just… disconnect."

"Exactly," Clara agreed, though she couldn't shake the feeling that there was more going on beneath the surface with Sarah and Daniel.

The conversation continued, but Clara found herself retreating into her thoughts. The storm outside had turned the inn into a world of its own, a snow globe where time seemed to slow down. It was what she had wanted—an escape, a chance to regroup. But the isolation, the quiet, it was starting to feel a little too intense, a little too close.

She shook her head, trying to clear it. Maybe she just needed some rest. The drive had been long, and the storm had frayed her nerves. A good night's sleep would make everything seem clearer in the morning.

"Excuse me," she said, rising from her chair. "I think I'm going to head up to my room. It's been a long day."

"Of course," Charles said, giving her a sympathetic smile.

"We'll see you at breakfast."

"Goodnight," Emma added, her voice soft.

"Goodnight," Clara replied, nodding to the group before heading for the stairs.

The hallway was quiet, the only sound the muffled roar of the wind outside. Clara made her way up to the second floor, where her room was located near the end of the hall. The room was just as she'd left it, warm and inviting, with the thick quilt folded neatly at the foot of the bed.

Clara closed the door behind her, leaning against it for a moment as she let out a long breath. The tension that had been building all evening seemed to dissipate slightly now that she was alone. She crossed the room to the window, pulling back the heavy curtain to peer out at the storm.

The snow was still coming down hard, but now it seemed almost peaceful, the flakes drifting down in a lazy, swirling dance. The world outside was a blank canvas, pure and untouched. For a moment, Clara allowed herself to believe that she could leave all her worries behind, that she could find some measure of peace in this remote mountain inn.

But as she watched the snow, she couldn't shake the feeling that something was lurking just beyond the edge of her awareness, something dark and unyielding, waiting for the right moment to emerge.

With a sigh, she turned away from the window and began to prepare for bed. She was tired, more tired than she'd realized, and all she wanted now was to crawl under the warm covers and let sleep take her.

As she settled into the bed, pulling the quilt up to her chin, Clara closed her eyes and tried to push all her worries aside. She was safe here, away from the noise and the chaos of the city. This was her chance to rest, to regroup, to figure out what came next.

But as she drifted off to sleep, the storm continued to rage outside, and the feeling of unease lingered, like a shadow at the edge of her dreams, refusing to be ignored.

2

Chapter 2

The storm had settled into a steady rhythm by the time Clara woke. The snow tapped against the window like a million tiny fingers, insistent but oddly soothing. She lay there for a moment, cocooned in the heavy quilt, the warmth of the bed seeping into her bones. For a fleeting moment, she felt a sense of peace, the kind that comes when you're far away from everything familiar, everything that weighs you down.

Then reality started to creep back in. She wasn't just here for a vacation. She was here to escape. Or at least, that's what she'd told herself. She pushed the thought away, not wanting to start her day with the same old doubts. Today was supposed to be different. Today was about finding some clarity, some direction. She forced herself out of bed, feet hitting the cold floor with a sharp reminder of the world outside.

A quick glance out the window showed nothing but white— snow still falling, the trees barely visible through the thick blanket of it. It would be easy to lose yourself here, to forget there was a world beyond the mountains. She dressed quickly, pulling on a thick sweater and jeans, then hesitated before grabbing her notebook. It was an old habit, bringing it everywhere, even when she wasn't working on anything specific. But the need to write, to process, was always there, lurking just beneath the surface.

Downstairs, the inn was quiet. The fire in the lounge had burned down to embers, and the smell of coffee wafted from the dining room. Clara followed the scent, finding Margaret setting out a simple breakfast—fresh bread, butter, jam, and a pot of coffee that steamed invitingly in the center of the table.

"Morning, Clara," Margaret said with a warm smile, as if they were old friends. "Sleep well?"

"Well enough," Clara replied, returning the smile. "That storm is something else."

Margaret nodded, her hands moving deftly as she arranged the table. "It's not letting up anytime soon, I'm afraid. But that's part of the charm, isn't it? Being snowed in, nowhere to go, nothing to do but relax."

"Yeah," Clara agreed, though the idea of being trapped here, even in such a beautiful place, made her a little uneasy. "I suppose it is."

"You're the second one down," Margaret continued, pouring coffee into a large mug and sliding it across the table. "But the others should be along soon. Help yourself to whatever you like."

Clara took the mug gratefully, wrapping her hands around it for warmth. "Thanks. This is just what I needed."

Margaret smiled again, that same calming expression that made Clara feel like everything was going to be okay, even when she wasn't sure it would be. "Take your time. There's no rush here." Margaret then proceeded to take the coffee and a few mugs in to the lounge.

Clara could hear the low murmur of voices from the lounge—a sign that the other guests were waking up, getting ready to start their day. She sipped on her coffee and wandered into the lounge, where Charles was already seated by the fire, reading a newspaper.

"Morning, Clara," he said without looking up, his voice as steady and reassuring as ever. "Sleep well?"

"Morning, Charles. Yeah, I did. You?"

"Always do here," he replied, folding the paper and setting it aside. "This place has a way of making everything seem a little less complicated."

Clara continued to sip her coffee, letting the warmth spread through her. "I hope so. That's why I'm here, after all."

Charles nodded, his gaze thoughtful. "Aren't we all? This inn draws people in when they need it most."

Before Clara could respond, Emma appeared in the doorway, looking as nervous as she had the night before. "Morning," she said quietly, hovering near the entrance like she wasn't sure if she was welcome.

"Morning, Emma," Charles said, gesturing to the chair next to him. "Come, sit. The coffee's hot, and I'm sure Margaret will have breakfast ready soon."

Emma hesitated, then moved to the chair, sitting down with a small sigh. "Thanks. I didn't sleep much. That storm… it's loud."

"It's always like that the first night," Charles said kindly. "But you'll get used to it. There's nothing to worry about here."

Emma offered a weak smile, but Clara could see the tension in her posture, the way her hands twisted together in her lap. She couldn't help but wonder what had brought Emma here, what she was running from—or maybe, what she was trying to find.

The sound of footsteps on the stairs drew Clara's attention, and she turned to see Sarah and Daniel descending, looking just as put together as they had the night before. Sarah's dark hair was pulled back into a sleek ponytail, and Daniel's crisp shirt looked like it had just been pressed.

"Morning," Daniel said, his voice clipped but polite. "How's everyone doing?"

"Good," Charles replied, ever the diplomat. "Just getting settled in. There's coffee in here, if you'd like some."

"Sounds perfect," Sarah said, her tone as smooth as her appearance. "This storm… it's something, isn't it?"

"It is," Clara said, watching the couple closely. There was something off about them, something she couldn't quite put her finger on. They were too polished, too controlled. In a place like this, it stood out.

Daniel and Sarah exchanged a glance, something unspoken passing between them. Then Daniel smiled, a little too brightly. "Well, it's a good excuse to relax, right? No distractions, no demands. Just peace and quiet."

"Exactly," Charles agreed, though his eyes flicked between the couple with the same curiosity Clara felt. "That's what we're all here for."

The group settled into a comfortable silence, the kind that comes when strangers are still feeling each other out, unsure of where they stand. Clara found herself relaxing slightly, the warmth of the fire and the coffee doing their job. It was strange, being here with these people, each of them so different, yet all drawn to the same place. There was a story behind each of them, she was sure of it.

Margaret appeared again, this time carrying a tray laden with fresh bread, butter, and jam. "Breakfast is ready," she announced, setting the tray on a small table near the fire. "Help yourselves. There's plenty to go around."

"Thank you, Margaret," Charles said, rising to pour himself another cup of coffee. "You're spoiling us."

Margaret laughed, a warm, genuine sound. "Just doing my job. Besides, there's not much else to do in this storm."

"That's true," Clara said, reaching for a slice of bread. "How long do you think it'll last?"

Margaret shrugged, a gesture that was both casual and resigned. "Could be a day, could be more. The mountains are unpredictable this time of year. But don't worry, we're well stocked. And the generator will keep us warm if the power goes out."

"Comforting," Sarah murmured, her tone suggesting the opposite.

Clara watched as Margaret smiled at Sarah, unruffled by her cool demeanor. "We've been through worse," Margaret said calmly. "You're in good hands."

The breakfast conversation was light, everyone sticking to safe topics—the storm, the beauty of the inn, their travel experiences. But Clara's mind was already working, trying to piece together the puzzle of these people. Charles, with his quiet wisdom, seemed genuine enough. Emma, nervous and jumpy, was clearly dealing with something deeper. And Sarah and Daniel… they were a mystery wrapped in an enigma, their polished exterior hiding something Clara couldn't yet see.

But she would see it. She always did, eventually.

The morning passed slowly, the storm outside showing no signs of stopping. Clara spent most of it in the lounge, alternating between reading and watching the snow fall outside. The others drifted in and out, each finding their own way to pass the time. Charles returned to his newspaper, Emma tried and failed to focus on a book, and Sarah and Daniel kept to themselves, speaking in low tones whenever they were alone together.

By midday, the snow was even heavier, the world outside a swirling mass of white. The wind howled, shaking the windows and sending a chill through the inn despite the roaring fire. Clara found herself feeling more restless, the walls of the inn starting to close in on her.

"Want to take a walk?" Charles asked, noticing her agitation. "Fresh air might do you good."

Clara hesitated, glancing out the window. The snow was piling up fast, but the idea of getting outside, even for a few minutes, was tempting. "Sure. If we don't get lost in the storm."

Charles chuckled. "We'll stick close to the inn. Just a quick loop around the building."

Clara nodded, grabbing her coat and scarf. "Let's do it."

They bundled up and stepped outside, the cold air hitting them like a slap. The snow was nearly knee-deep now, and the wind whipped it around them in fierce gusts. But the fresh air was invigorating, and Clara found herself smiling as they trudged through the drifts.

"It's beautiful, isn't it?" Charles said, his voice muffled by his scarf.

"It is," Clara agreed, her breath fogging in the cold air. "But I'm glad we're not going far."

They walked in silence for a while, the only sounds the crunch of snow beneath their boots and the howling of the wind. The inn looked even more isolated in the storm, the building almost swallowed up by the snow. But there was something comforting about it, too. A safe haven in the middle of the wilderness.

"So," Charles said after a while, breaking the silence. "What are you hoping to find here, Clara?"

Clara glanced at him, surprised by the question. "I don't know, really. I just needed to get away. Clear my head."

"From what?"

She hesitated, not sure how much she wanted to share. But there was something about Charles, something steady and trustworthy, that made her want to open up. "I lost my job," she admitted finally. "A job I cared about. And now I don't know what's next."

Charles nodded, his expression thoughtful. "That's tough. But sometimes losing something makes room for something better."

"I hope so," Clara said, though her voice was tinged with doubt. "I just… I don't know where to start."

"Maybe you don't have to," Charles said, his tone gentle. "Maybe you just need to let things be for a while. See what comes to you."

Clara considered that, her breath coming in little puffs as they walked. "Maybe."

They completed their loop around the inn and headed back inside, the warmth of the fire a welcome relief after the biting cold. Clara felt a little better, the walk having cleared some of the cobwebs from her mind. But there was still that lingering feeling, that sense that something wasn't quite right.

The rest of the day passed in much the same way. The group stayed mostly in the lounge, making small talk, reading, and occasionally braving the storm for fresh air. But as the afternoon wore on, the atmosphere began to change. The novelty of the storm was wearing off, and the reality of being snowed in was starting to set in. The walls seemed to close in a little more with each passing hour.

By evening, the storm was at its peak. The wind howled outside, rattling the windows and shaking the walls. The fire in the lounge was burning brightly, but the warmth didn't seem to reach Clara the way it had earlier. The unease she'd been feeling all day had settled in her chest, a heavy weight that refused to go away.

Margaret served dinner—a simple, hearty meal of stew and bread—but the conversation around the table was stilted, the tension in the room almost palpable. Even Charles seemed more subdued, his usual calm demeanor giving way to a quiet introspection.

"Do you think the storm will let up soon?" Emma asked, her voice small, almost childlike.

"It's hard to say," Margaret replied, her tone calm but firm. "But we're safe here. The inn is well-stocked, and the generator will keep us warm if the power goes out."She repeated.

"That's good," Emma murmured, though she didn't look reassured.

Sarah and Daniel exchanged another one of their silent looks, the kind that made Clara's skin prickle with suspicion. There was something about them, something they were hiding. She was sure of it.

After dinner, the group settled back into the lounge, but the mood had shifted. The earlier camaraderie was gone, replaced by a tense silence that hung over them like a thick fog. Clara tried to read, but she couldn't focus, her mind too busy turning over everything that had happened, everything that felt off.

Eventually, Margaret suggested they all turn in for the night, and Clara was relieved. She needed space, needed to be alone with her thoughts. She said goodnight to the others and made her way back to her room, her footsteps echoing in the quiet hallway.

In the safety of her room, she let out a long breath, trying to shake off the tension that had been building all day. She changed into her pajamas and crawled into bed, but sleep didn't come easily. The storm outside was louder than ever, the wind howling like a living thing, clawing at the walls and windows.

As she lay there in the dark, listening to the storm, that sense of unease grew stronger, creeping into the edges of her mind. Something wasn't right. She didn't know what it was, but she could feel it, like a shadow lurking just out of sight.

Clara closed her eyes, trying to push the thoughts away, but they wouldn't leave. The storm outside was relentless, pounding against the inn, and inside her mind, a different kind of storm was brewing—one that she couldn't escape, no matter how hard she tried.

She rolled over, pulling the covers tighter around her, but sleep was elusive. The minutes ticked by, and the storm continued, unyielding and merciless. The unease in her chest grew heavier, a weight that pressed down on her, making it hard to breathe.

Eventually, exhaustion took over, and Clara drifted into a restless sleep, her dreams haunted by shadows and whispers she couldn't quite understand. The storm raged on, and with it, the sense that something was terribly, terribly wrong.

3

Chapter 3

Clara woke to silence. The kind of silence that felt heavy, almost unnatural. She lay still, blinking up at the ceiling, trying to orient herself. The storm had been so loud, so fierce, but now… nothing. Not a whisper of wind, not a creak from the walls. Just the thick, oppressive quiet that made her feel like she was buried deep underground.

She pushed the covers aside and sat up, the cold air hitting her skin like a shock. The fire in the small hearth had gone out during the night, leaving the room chilled. She rubbed her arms, trying to chase away the goosebumps, and glanced out the window.

Snow. Still snowing, but slower now, the flakes drifting lazily to the ground. The world outside was a sea of white, the trees heavy with the burden of it. It was beautiful, in a way that made her chest chest feel warm. And also isolating. Suffocating.

Clara dressed quickly, pulling on the warmest clothes she had. She wasn't sure what time it was—her phone was dead, and the small clock on the nightstand had stopped ticking sometime in the night—but it felt early. The kind of early where everything still feels half asleep, the world not yet fully awake.

She needed coffee. Something to shake off the last remnants of her uneasy sleep, to push away the shadows that had lingered in her dreams. She grabbed her notebook and headed downstairs, hoping the others were still asleep so she could have a moment alone.

But as she reached the bottom of the stairs, she heard voices. Low, tense. Not the friendly, easy chatter of the day before. This was different, and it made her pause, listening.

"…can't just show up like that," a voice—Daniel's, she thought—said, tight with irritation.

"What choice did he have?" That was Charles, calm as ever, but there was an edge to his voice, something Clara hadn't heard before. "The storm was bad. He would've frozen out there."

"It's just… weird," Emma said, her voice small. "Like, why was he out there in the first place?"

Clara's curiosity piqued. She stepped quietly into the hallway, moving closer to the lounge where the voices were coming from.

"I don't trust him," Sarah's voice cut in, sharp and clipped. "We don't know anything about him. He could be anyone."

"We're all strangers here," Charles said, trying to placate her. "Doesn't mean he's a threat."

"Doesn't mean he isn't," Daniel shot back.

Clara rounded the corner into the lounge. Four pairs of eyes snapped to her as she entered, the tension in the room thick enough to cut with a knife. Charles was sitting in his usual chair by the fire, Emma perched nervously on the edge of the sofa. Sarah and Daniel stood near the window, their postures stiff, defensive.

"What's going on?" Clara asked, trying to sound casual as she took in the scene.

"An unexpected guest," Charles said with a slight smile, but it didn't reach his eyes. "He showed up late last night. In the middle of the storm."

Clara blinked. "What?"

"He was out there," Emma said, her voice trembling slightly. "Knocked on the door, said his car broke down and he got caught in the storm."

"Margaret let him in," Charles added, his tone neutral. "Didn't have much choice. The storm was too bad."

Clara processed that, glancing around the room. "Where is he now?"

"Margaret gave him a room," Charles said. "She's with him now, getting him settled."

"What's he like?" Clara asked, trying to mask her unease. The idea of someone new, someone unplanned, unsettled her more than she wanted to admit.

Sarah crossed her arms, her expression cold. "He's… odd. Quiet. Didn't say much, just that he needed shelter."

"Which is exactly what anyone would say in that situation," Charles pointed out.

"Or what someone pretending to need shelter would say," Daniel muttered.

Clara frowned. "What do you mean?"

Daniel exchanged a look with Sarah before answering. "He was way too calm. Too put together for someone who just wandered in from a storm like that. Didn't even look that cold."

"He had a coat," Charles said, still trying to keep the peace. "And we don't know how long he was out there."

"I don't like it," Sarah said flatly. "We don't know him. And now we're all stuck here together."

Clara felt a shiver run down her spine, and it wasn't from the cold. The inn had felt safe before, even with the storm raging outside. But now… something had shifted. The presence of a stranger changed everything, and not for the better.

She opened her mouth to respond, but before she could, Margaret appeared in the doorway. She looked tired, more so than Clara had seen before. Her smile was strained, but she tried to project the same warmth she always did.

"Morning, everyone," she said, her voice too bright. "I see you've all heard about our new guest."

"Hard not to," Daniel muttered.

Margaret's eyes flicked to him, but she ignored the comment. "His name is Alex Matthews. He's a writer, traveling through the area. Got caught in the storm when his car broke down. Poor man was half-frozen when he got here."

"Is he okay?" Emma asked, her voice soft, concerned.

"He's fine," Margaret assured her. "Just needs some rest. I've set him up in the room at the end of the hall."

"Great," Sarah said, her tone flat. "Another mouth to feed."

Margaret's smile wavered, just a bit. "We have plenty of supplies. And it's Christmas, after all. The more, the merrier."

But no one looked particularly merry. The tension in the room was palpable, and Clara could tell that Margaret was struggling to keep control of the situation.

"Let's not jump to conclusions," Margaret said, her tone more firm now. "Alex is just another guest, like all of you. He needed help, and we provided it. That's what decent people do."

Clara felt a pang of guilt. Margaret was right. They were all strangers here, brought together by circumstance. Just because this Alex had arrived unexpectedly didn't mean he was a threat. But still, something about the situation didn't sit right with her.

"Maybe we should meet him," Clara suggested, trying to ease the tension. "Get to know him a bit. It might make everyone feel more comfortable."

Margaret's smile returned, though it was still a bit strained. "That's a good idea, Clara. I'm sure Alex would appreciate that."

But the others didn't seem convinced. Sarah's arms remained crossed, her expression icy. Daniel didn't meet Clara's eyes, and Emma looked like she wanted to shrink into the couch and disappear.

Charles, ever the diplomat, cleared his throat. "I think that's a fine idea. We're all stuck here together for the foreseeable future. We might as well make the best of it."

Margaret nodded, relieved to have someone on her side. "I'll go check on him. See if he's feeling up to joining us for breakfast."

She left the room, and an awkward silence followed. Clara could feel the weight of everyone's unease pressing down on her, making it hard to breathe.

"This is going to be a disaster," Sarah muttered, her voice low enough that only Daniel and Clara could hear. "I can feel it."

Daniel didn't respond, but the look on his face said he agreed.

Clara didn't know what to say, so she stayed quiet, sipping her coffee and staring into the fire. The flames danced and flickered, casting long shadows on the walls. It should have been comforting, but it wasn't. Not anymore.

After a few minutes, Margaret returned, and with her was a man—presumably Alex Matthews. He was tall, with a lean build and dark hair that was just starting to show the first signs of gray. He had a calm, almost serene expression on his face, but there was something in his eyes that made Clara uneasy. They were too sharp, too watchful, like he was constantly analyzing everything around him.

"Everyone, this is Alex," Margaret said, her tone cheerful but with an underlying note of tension. "Alex, these are our other guests: Charles, Emma, Sarah, Daniel, and Clara."

Alex nodded politely, his eyes moving over each of them in turn. "Nice to meet you all," he said, his voice smooth, almost too smooth. "Sorry to barge in like this. I know it's not ideal."

"You were stuck in a storm," Charles said, ever the peacemaker. "You did what you had to do. No need to apologize."

Alex smiled, but it didn't seem genuine. "Thanks. I appreciate that."

Another awkward silence followed, and Clara found herself wishing she was anywhere else. The tension in the room was suffocating, the unease thickening with every passing second.

"So, you're a writer?" Emma asked, breaking the silence with a voice that trembled slightly.

"Yes," Alex replied, turning his gaze to her. "I travel a lot, looking for inspiration. This part of the country is… quite inspiring."

Clara watched him closely, trying to gauge his sincerity. But he was hard to read, his expression calm and composed, revealing nothing. She didn't like it. She didn't like him.

"Well," Margaret said, clapping her hands together in an attempt to break the tension. "Breakfast is ready, and I'm sure we could all use some food. Why don't we sit down and eat?"

The group moved toward the dining room, but the atmosphere remained tense. Clara found herself sitting across from Alex, and the proximity made her skin crawl. She couldn't put her finger on why, but something about him set off all her internal alarms.

The conversation during breakfast was stilted, each attempt at small talk falling flat. Alex answered questions politely, but his responses were short, almost rehearsed, as if he were playing a part rather than genuinely engaging. Every time Clara tried to catch his eye, he seemed to look right through her, like she wasn't even there.

"You said your car broke down?" Daniel asked suddenly, his tone challenging.

Alex nodded, unperturbed by the suspicion in Daniel's voice. "Yes, the engine just… died. I was lucky to find this place when I did."

"Lucky," Sarah echoed, her voice flat.

Alex smiled, but it was a thin, cold smile. "I'd say so."

The rest of the meal passed in strained silence. Clara picked at her food, appetite gone, and kept stealing glances at Alex. There was something about him that was off, something she couldn't shake. He was too calm, too composed. Like he was playing a role, and they were all his unwitting audience.

Finally, the meal ended, and the group dispersed. Clara found herself alone in the lounge, staring into the dying embers of the fire. The unease that had been building all morning was now a steady thrum in her chest, a warning she couldn't ignore.

She heard footsteps behind her and turned to see Charles approaching, his expression thoughtful. "You're worried about him too," he said quietly, not a question, but a statement.

Clara nodded, feeling a rush of relief that she wasn't the only one. "Yeah. I don't know why, but… something's not right."

Charles sighed, rubbing a hand over his face. "I agree. But we're stuck with him for now. We just have to keep an eye on him, make sure nothing… happens."

Clara swallowed, her mouth dry. "What do you think he wants?"

"I don't know," Charles admitted, his voice heavy with concern. "But whatever it is, I don't think it's good."

They fell silent, the weight of their shared unease settling over them like a blanket. The fire crackled softly, the only sound in the room, but it did little to dispel the cold that had seeped into Clara's bones.

As the day wore on, the tension in the inn grew thicker. Alex kept to himself, spending most of his time in his room or taking short walks around the building. But even when he wasn't present, his presence loomed large, casting a shadow over everything.

Margaret did her best to keep things normal, to maintain a sense of calm, but even she couldn't hide the worry in her eyes. The storm outside had weakened, but the one inside the inn was just beginning to brew.

By evening, the group was on edge. No one spoke much, and when they did, it was with forced cheerfulness that fooled no one. Clara found herself retreating into her thoughts, trying to figure out what it was about Alex that made her so uneasy. She didn't have an answer, but the feeling wouldn't go away.

That night, Clara lay awake in bed, listening to the wind howling outside. The storm was picking up again, a fresh wave of snow beating against the windows. But it wasn't the storm that kept her awake. It was the feeling that something was very, very wrong.

She rolled over, pulling the covers tight around her, but sleep wouldn't come. The inn felt different now, less like a refuge and more like a trap. And she couldn't shake the feeling that they were all in danger, that Alex's arrival had changed everything.

Hours passed, and still she lay there, wide awake, heart pounding in the silence. She thought of getting up, of finding Charles or Margaret, but something held her back. The fear that if she left her room, something terrible would happen. That the thin walls of her room were the only thing keeping her safe.

Finally, exhaustion took over, and Clara drifted into a fitful sleep, her dreams haunted by shadows and the feeling of being watched. The storm raged on, and with it, the certainty that their unwanted visitor was not who he claimed to be.

4

Chapter 4

The smell of coffee drew Clara from the shallow, restless sleep she'd finally fallen into. She blinked groggily at the ceiling, disoriented, the remnants of unsettling dreams clinging to her mind like cobwebs. The storm had quieted overnight, leaving behind a deep, eerie stillness that made the inn feel even more isolated.

Pushing the covers aside, she sat up, the cold air prickling her skin. She hesitated before getting out of bed, that familiar sense of unease still coiled in her stomach. Alex's arrival had thrown everything off balance, and the tension among the guests was thick enough to taste.

She dressed quickly, layering on clothes against the morning chill, and made her way downstairs. The inn was quiet, the only sound the soft murmur of voices from the dining room. As she approached, she could make out the familiar tones of Charles and Margaret, along with a third voice—Alex's.

She paused just outside the door, listening.

"…think the storm's let up enough for me to get a signal?" Alex was saying, his voice calm and measured.

"Hard to say," Margaret replied, a trace of unease in her tone. "The mountains play tricks on the signals out here. But you're welcome to try."

Clara frowned, her fingers tightening on the edge of the doorframe. She couldn't shake the feeling that Alex was too calm, too composed. Most people would be anxious, restless after a night like that. But not him. No, he seemed perfectly at ease, like he belonged here. Like he'd planned it all along.

"Morning," she said, stepping into the dining room before she could second-guess herself.

Three pairs of eyes turned to her as she entered. Charles gave her a nod, his expression guarded. Margaret smiled. And Alex… well, his face remained impassive, his eyes sharp and assessing as they locked onto hers.

"Morning, Clara," Margaret said, her tone forced-cheerful. "Coffee's fresh, and there's some toast and eggs if you're hungry."

Clara nodded, but her appetite was nonexistent. "Thanks." She poured herself a cup of coffee and took a seat at the table, trying to ignore the way Alex's gaze followed her every move.

"Looks like the storm's finally easing up," Charles said, his voice breaking the awkward silence. "Might be able to get out of here soon."

"I hope so," Clara murmured, though the idea of leaving didn't bring as much relief as she thought it would. "What's the plan, Margaret? Are the roads passable?"

"Not yet," Margaret replied, her expression tightening slightly. "We'll have to wait for the plows, and that might take a while. The main roads are their priority. We're a bit… out of the way."

Alex sipped his coffee, his movements slow, deliberate.

"We'll just have to make the best of it then."

Clara suppressed a shiver. There was something about the way he said it, like he was savoring the situation. Like he wanted them to stay trapped here a little longer.

Margaret nodded, but the tension in her posture didn't go unnoticed. "Yes, well, let's hope the plows come through sooner rather than later. In the meantime, we'll keep the fire going and make sure everyone stays warm."

Charles glanced at Clara, his expression unreadable. "How'd you sleep?"

"Not great," Clara admitted, sipping her coffee to avoid meeting his eyes. "Just… restless, I guess."

Alex set his cup down with a soft clink, his gaze fixed on her. "Storms like that have a way of getting under your skin. Makes you feel… unsettled."

Clara looked up, meeting his eyes for a brief moment before looking away. "Yeah. Something like that."

Another awkward silence descended over the table, the tension thickening with each passing second. Clara felt like she was suffocating under the weight of it, the air in the room too heavy, too close. She needed to get out of there, needed some fresh air, even if it was freezing.

"I think I'll take a walk," she said abruptly, pushing her chair back and standing up. "Clear my head."

"Mind if I join you?" Charles asked, his tone casual, but Clara could see the concern in his eyes.

She hesitated, then nodded. "Sure."

They left the dining room together, the silence between them more comfortable than the strained conversation inside. As they stepped out into the lobby, Charles spoke up, his voice low.

"Something's not right about him."

Clara glanced at him, her heart skipping a beat. "You feel it too?"

Charles nodded, his expression grim. "I've been around long enough to trust my gut, and it's telling me that man is trouble."

Clara swallowed, her mouth suddenly dry. "But what can we do? We're stuck here with him."

"For now," Charles said, his tone steady. "But we don't have to trust him. We just have to keep our wits about us, stay on guard."

Clara nodded, the knot of anxiety in her stomach tightening. "Do you think Margaret knows?"

Charles sighed, rubbing a hand over his face. "I think she's trying to keep everyone calm, keep things under control. But she's no fool. She knows something's off."

Clara's mind raced as they stepped outside into the cold, crisp air. The snow had stopped, but the world was still blanketed in white, the trees heavy with the weight of it. The inn looked almost picturesque, a postcard image of winter tranquility. But the tension inside shattered that illusion.

They walked in silence for a while, the only sound the crunch of snow beneath their boots. Clara kept stealing glances at Charles, trying to gauge his thoughts. He was a steady presence, calm and composed, but there was a weariness in his eyes that spoke of experience. He'd seen things, been through things. And now, she realized, he was taking on the role of protector, trying to keep everyone safe.

"Have you talked to the others?" Clara asked, her breath fogging in the cold air.

"Not directly," Charles replied, his tone careful. "But I think Emma's scared, more than she's letting on. Sarah and Daniel…

they're harder to read. But I get the feeling they're hiding something too."

Clara bit her lip, her thoughts churning. "What do we do?"

Charles stopped walking, turning to face her. "We watch. We listen. And if something doesn't feel right, we act."

Clara nodded, the weight of responsibility settling heavily on her shoulders. She wasn't used to this, wasn't used to being in a situation where her instincts were her only guide. But she trusted Charles. And she trusted her own gut, which was screaming at her that Alex was dangerous.

They continued their walk, circling the inn before heading back inside. The cold had cleared Clara's head a bit, but the unease lingered, like a shadow that wouldn't go away. When they reentered the inn, they found Margaret in the lobby, her expression tight.

"Everything okay?" Charles asked, his tone casual but with an undercurrent of concern.

Margaret forced a smile. "Just checking the supplies. We have enough to last us a while, but I'd rather not be stuck here longer than necessary."

Clara glanced around, noticing that the lounge was empty. "Where's Alex?"

Margaret's smile faltered slightly. "In his room, I believe. Said he needed to rest."

Charles exchanged a look with Clara before turning back to Margaret. "And the others?"

"Emma's in her room too," Margaret replied. "Sarah and Daniel went out for a walk, I think."

"Alone?" Clara asked, frowning.

Margaret nodded, her expression unreadable. "They seemed to want some privacy."

Clara's unease deepened, but she didn't press the issue. Instead, she turned to Charles. "Maybe we should check on Emma. She seemed pretty shaken up earlier."

"Good idea," Charles agreed. "You go ahead, I'll be right behind you."

Clara nodded and made her way up the stairs, the old wood creaking underfoot. The hallway was dimly lit, the shadows long and deep. She reached Emma's door and hesitated, raising her hand to knock.

Before she could, the door creaked open, and Emma's pale face appeared in the gap. "Clara," she said, her voice barely above a whisper. "What's going on?"

Clara gave her a reassuring smile, though it felt forced. "Just checking in. How are you holding up?"

Emma's eyes darted down the hall, as if she was expecting someone to jump out at her. "I don't know," she admitted, her voice trembling. "Something doesn't feel right."

Clara nodded, her own fears echoed in Emma's words. "I know. We just need to stay calm, stay together."

Emma opened the door wider, her expression pleading. "Can you come in? Just for a bit?"

Clara hesitated, then nodded. "Of course."

She stepped inside, noting the way Emma's hands shook as she closed the door behind her. The room was small but cozy, the bed neatly made, a book lying open on the nightstand. Emma moved to sit on the edge of the bed, her hands fidgeting in her lap.

"What are we going to do?" Emma asked, her voice barely above a whisper.

Clara sat down in the chair by the window, keeping her tone calm. "We're going to be careful. Charles and I will keep an eye on things. But we need you to stay strong, okay? Don't let fear take over."

Emma nodded, though her eyes were still wide with fear. "It's just… he gives me the creeps. I don't trust him."

"Neither do I," Clara admitted, leaning forward slightly. "But we're not alone. We've got each other, and we've got Margaret and Charles. We'll get through this."

Emma took a deep breath, trying to steady herself. "Okay. I'll try."

Clara gave her a reassuring smile. "That's all we can do."

They sat in silence for a few minutes, the weight of their situation hanging heavy in the air. Finally, Emma broke the silence, her voice soft and hesitant.

"Do you think… do you think he's dangerous?"

Clara didn't answer right away. She didn't want to lie, but she also didn't want to fuel Emma's fear. "I don't know," she said finally. "But we're going to be careful, okay? We won't take any chances."

Emma nodded, though the fear in her eyes didn't lessen. "Okay."

Clara stood up, forcing a smile. "I'll check in on you later, all right? Just… try to relax. Read your book, distract yourself."

Emma nodded again, but Clara could see that the words were little more than a comfort she couldn't quite grasp.

When Clara left Emma's room, Charles was waiting in the hall, his expression somber. "How is she?" he asked quietly.

"Scared," Clara replied. "But she's holding it together."

Charles nodded, his eyes flicking down the hallway. "We should talk to Margaret. Come up with a plan, just in case."

"Agreed," Clara said, following him down the stairs.

When they found Margaret in the lobby, she was sitting

by the fire, staring into the flames. She looked up as they approached, her expression weary. "How's Emma?" she asked, her voice tinged with concern.

"Scared," Clara said. "But she'll be okay."

Margaret sighed, rubbing her temples. "This is a mess. I don't know what to do."

Charles sat down beside her, his tone gentle. "We need to be prepared. Just in case."

Margaret nodded, though she still looked overwhelmed. "What are you suggesting?"

"Nothing drastic," Charles said quickly. "But we need to make sure everyone's safe. That means keeping an eye on Alex, sticking together, and making sure no one's alone for too long."

Margaret looked down at her hands, her brow furrowed. "I don't want to jump to conclusions. But you're right. We need to be cautious."

Clara took a seat across from them, her mind racing. "Do you have any way to contact the outside world? In case… in case we need help?"

Margaret shook her head, her expression grim. "The landline's out, and cell service is spotty at best. We're on our own for now."

Clara's heart sank, the reality of their situation settling over her like a lead weight. They were trapped, with no way to call for help if things went wrong. The inn, once a refuge, now felt like a prison.

"What about the generator?" Charles asked, his voice steady.

"It's working," Margaret said. "We're not going to freeze, if that's what you're worried about."

Charles nodded, but his eyes were dark with worry. "Good. Let's just keep everyone together, keep things as normal as possible. We don't want to raise any alarms, not until we have to."

Clara and Margaret both nodded in agreement, but the unease remained. They were playing a dangerous game, walking a fine line between caution and paranoia. And one misstep could mean disaster.

As the day wore on, the tension only grew. The guests kept to their rooms for the most part, emerging only for meals or brief walks around the inn. Alex remained a ghost, slipping in and out of rooms with an unsettling quietness that made Clara's skin crawl. Every time she saw him, that feeling of unease sharpened, a blade pressed against her spine.

The snow outside continued to fall, but lighter now, the world slowly being buried under a thick blanket of white. The isolation was complete, the outside world a distant memory.

By evening, Clara was exhausted, her nerves frayed from the constant tension. She found herself in the lounge once again, staring into the fire, trying to make sense of the chaos in her mind. Charles sat beside her, his presence a steadying force.

"We'll get through this," he said quietly, his voice calm and reassuring.

Clara nodded, though the fear still gnawed at her. "I hope you're right."

"I am," Charles said, his tone firm. "We just need to stick together."

They sat in silence for a while, the fire crackling softly beside them. The inn was quiet, the only sounds the occasional creak of the old building and the faint rustle of wind outside.

But Clara couldn't shake the feeling that this was just the calm before the storm. That something was coming, something they couldn't see, but could feel in their bones.

And when it came, they would have to be ready. Because if they weren't, they might not survive.

5

Chapter 5

The day dragged on, each minute feeling like an hour. The storm outside had reduced to a faint whisper of wind, the snow falling so lightly it was almost imperceptible. Inside, the atmosphere was heavy, as if the very walls of the inn were closing in on them. Clara couldn't shake the feeling that they were all teetering on the edge of something, but she didn't know what.

The unease settled deep in her bones, a constant companion that refused to leave her side. She found herself pacing the hallways, the steady rhythm of her footsteps on the creaking floorboards the only thing keeping her grounded. Each time she passed by Alex's door, she slowed, listening for any sound from within. But there was nothing. Just silence.

She tried to distract herself, but it was useless. Her thoughts kept circling back to the same place, the same worry: Alex. Who was he? What did he want? Why was he really here?

And most importantly, how could they protect themselves from him if it came to that?

Clara wandered into the lounge, where Charles was sitting

by the fire, a book open in his lap. But he wasn't reading. His eyes were unfocused, staring into the flames as if searching for answers. He looked up when she entered, giving her a small, weary smile.

"Can't sit still, can you?" he asked, his tone gentle.

Clara shook her head, the tension in her shoulders refusing to ease. "I can't stop thinking."

"About him?"

"Yeah," Clara admitted, sinking into the chair across from him. "I don't trust him, Charles. There's something off."

Charles nodded, closing his book and setting it aside. "I agree. But we have to be careful. We can't let our suspicions turn into something dangerous."

Clara frowned, her hands fidgeting in her lap. "But what if he's planning something? What if—"

"Let's not get ahead of ourselves," Charles interrupted, his voice calm but firm. "We don't know anything for sure. We need to stay vigilant, yes, but we can't let fear cloud our judgment."

Clara sighed, leaning back in her chair. "I just wish I knew what he was thinking. What he's hiding."

"Maybe we'll find out sooner than we think," Charles said, his eyes dark with concern.

Clara didn't respond. The fire crackled between them, its warmth doing little to chase away the chill that had settled in her chest. They sat in silence for a while, both lost in their own thoughts, until the sound of footsteps broke the quiet.

Sarah and Daniel appeared in the doorway, their expressions tight. Sarah's eyes were sharp, scanning the room as if she expected something—or someone—to jump out at her. Daniel's jaw was clenched, his hands stuffed into his pockets.

"We need to talk," Sarah said, her voice low and urgent.

Clara exchanged a glance with Charles before nodding. "Okay. What's going on?"

Sarah hesitated, glancing at Daniel, who nodded slightly, as if giving her permission to speak. "We've been keeping an eye on Alex," she began, her voice barely above a whisper. "And… we found something."

Clara's heart skipped a beat. "What do you mean? What did you find?"

Sarah stepped further into the room, her expression serious. "In his room. When he went out for a walk earlier, we… we searched it."

Clara's eyes widened, and even Charles looked surprised. "You searched his room?" Clara repeated, her voice incredulous. "Why?"

"Because something isn't right," Daniel said, his tone defensive. "You've all felt it too, haven't you? We needed to know."

Clara's mind raced, trying to process what they were saying. "What did you find?"

Sarah glanced around, as if making sure no one else was listening, before stepping closer to Clara and Charles. "He has a gun."

The words hung in the air like a lead weight, sinking into Clara's stomach with a sickening thud. She stared at Sarah, trying to make sense of what she was hearing. "A gun?"

Sarah nodded, her expression grim. "It was in his bag, hidden under some clothes. It's small, but it's loaded. And there's more."

Clara felt her heart rate spike, her hands trembling slightly. "More?"

"Papers," Daniel said, his voice tight. "Documents. They're…

I don't know what they are exactly, but they're official-looking. Government or something. And there's a photo of someone. A woman. But it's not… it's not good."

Clara swallowed hard, her throat suddenly dry. "What do you mean?"

"It's like a surveillance photo," Sarah explained, her voice shaking slightly. "Black and white, grainy. The kind you see in spy movies. And the woman in the photo… she looks scared. Like she's running from something."

Clara felt a cold sweat break out on her forehead. This was worse than she'd imagined. Much worse. "What the hell is he doing with a gun and surveillance photos?"

"I don't know," Sarah admitted, her voice trembling. "But it's not good. Whatever it is, it's not good."

Charles, who had been silent during the exchange, finally spoke up, his voice steady but laced with concern. "We need to be careful. We don't know what we're dealing with."

"Careful?" Daniel scoffed, his tone bitter. "We should confront him. Get some answers."

"Confront him?" Clara echoed, her voice rising in panic. "And then what? What if he pulls the gun? What if he—"

"Clara's right," Charles said, cutting her off. "We can't just go charging in. We need a plan. We need to think this through."

Sarah nodded, though her eyes were still filled with fear. "What do we do then? Just wait? Hope he doesn't do anything?"

"We watch him," Charles said firmly. "We keep an eye on him, see if he makes a move. But we don't confront him. Not yet."

Clara's mind was spinning, the weight of the situation pressing down on her. This wasn't supposed to happen. They were supposed to be safe here, away from the chaos of the world. But now… now they were trapped with a man who was hiding a gun and God knows what else.

"What about Margaret?" Clara asked suddenly, her voice shaky. "Does she know?"

Sarah shook her head. "We haven't told her. Not yet."

"We should," Charles said, his tone decisive. "She needs to know what's going on."

"Right," Clara agreed, though the thought of dragging Margaret into this mess made her stomach turn. But they had no choice. They couldn't keep something like this from her. Not when it could mean the difference between life and death.

They found Margaret in the kitchen, preparing lunch. The smell of soup filled the air, but it did nothing to calm Clara's nerves. If anything, it made her feel sick. The idea of sitting down to a meal, pretending everything was normal, when there was a man with a gun just a few rooms away…

"Margaret," Charles began, his voice gentle but serious. "We need to talk."

Margaret looked up from the stove, her brow furrowed in concern. "What is it? What's wrong?"

"It's about Alex," Sarah said quietly, glancing around as if she was afraid he might walk in at any moment.

Margaret's eyes widened, and she set down the spoon she'd been holding. "What about him?"

Charles explained quickly, keeping his voice low. He told her about the gun, the papers, the surveillance photo. By the time he finished, Margaret's face had gone pale, her hands trembling slightly.

"I can't believe this," she whispered, her voice shaky. "Why would he…? What is he…?"

"We don't know," Clara said, her voice filled with a mixture of fear and frustration. "But we need to be careful. We can't confront him, not until we know more."

Margaret nodded slowly, her eyes filled with worry. "You're right. We have to be cautious."

Charles stepped forward, placing a reassuring hand on her shoulder. "We'll get through this, Margaret. But we need to stick together. We need to be smart."

Margaret took a deep breath, trying to steady herself. "Okay. Okay. We'll keep an eye on him. But what if… what if he does something? What if—"

"We'll handle it," Charles said firmly. "But we have to be ready."

The rest of the day passed in a blur of tension and anxiety. The guests moved around the inn like ghosts, their nerves frayed, their eyes darting to every shadow, every creak in the floorboards. Alex remained in his room for most of the day, only emerging briefly for meals, his demeanor as calm and composed as ever.

Clara watched him closely during dinner, her heart pounding with every bite of food she forced down. She kept expecting him to pull the gun, to make some kind of move. But he didn't. He just ate quietly, his eyes occasionally flicking around the room, as if assessing the situation.

After dinner, Clara found herself back in the lounge, her nerves on edge. She couldn't sit still, couldn't focus. The fear was a constant thrum in her chest, a relentless pressure that refused to let up. She needed to do something, anything, to keep herself from spiraling into panic.

Charles joined her after a while, his expression grim. "He's too calm," he said quietly, his eyes fixed on the fire. "Like he's waiting for something."

"I know," Clara replied, her voice barely above a whisper. "It's like he's playing a game, and we're all just… pieces."

Charles didn't respond, but the tension in his posture spoke volumes. They were all on edge, waiting for the other shoe to drop, for the storm to break.

And then it did.

It was late, the inn cloaked in darkness, the only light coming from the dim glow of the fire. Most of the guests had retired to their rooms, but Clara remained in the lounge, her nerves too frayed to sleep. Charles had gone up to check on Emma, leaving Clara alone with her thoughts.

That's when she heard it.

A muffled thud, followed by the sound of something—or someone—moving quickly down the hallway. Clara froze, her heart leaping into her throat. The noise had come from upstairs, near the guest rooms.

She stood up slowly, her hands trembling, and made her way to the bottom of the stairs. She strained to listen, her ears picking up every creak, every faint whisper of sound. There it was again—a soft rustle, a shuffling footstep.

Clara's breath hitched, fear coursing through her veins. She glanced around, her mind racing. Should she go up there? Should she find Charles? What if it was Alex? What if… what if someone was hurt?

Before she could decide, a figure appeared at the top of the stairs, silhouetted in the dim light. Clara's heart skipped a beat, her body tensing with fear. But then the figure stepped forward, and she let out a shaky breath.

It was Emma.

She looked pale, her eyes wide with fear. She was clutching

something in her hand, something small and metallic that glinted in the faint light.

"Emma?" Clara called out softly, her voice trembling. "What are you doing?"

Emma didn't respond. She just stared at Clara, her eyes filled with something Clara couldn't quite identify. It wasn't just fear. It was something deeper, something darker.

Clara took a hesitant step forward, her heart pounding. "Emma, what's wrong? What's going on?"

Emma's grip on the object in her hand tightened, her knuckles white. "I… I heard something," she whispered, her voice barely audible. "In his room. I think… I think he's gone."

"Gone?" Clara echoed, her mind struggling to catch up. "What do you mean?"

Emma swallowed hard, her eyes flicking nervously down the hallway. "He's not there. I… I checked. His room is empty."

Clara's blood ran cold. If Alex wasn't in his room… where was he?

Before she could say anything else, a loud crash echoed through the inn, the sound shattering the silence like a gunshot. Clara and Emma both jumped, their eyes wide with terror.

"That came from the kitchen," Clara whispered, her voice barely above a breath.

Without thinking, Clara grabbed Emma's hand, pulling her down the stairs. They moved quickly, their footsteps silent on the old wooden floors. Clara's mind raced, her heart pounding in her ears. What was happening? Where was Alex? What was going on?

They reached the kitchen, the door slightly ajar, the faint glow of moonlight spilling in through the window. Clara pushed the door open, her breath catching in her throat.

The kitchen was a mess. Pots and pans were scattered across the floor, the contents of the cabinets strewn everywhere. But what caught Clara's attention wasn't the mess. It was the back door. It was wide open, the cold night air seeping in.

And standing in the doorway was Alex.

He turned slowly, his eyes locking onto Clara's with a look that sent a shiver down her spine. There was something in his expression, something dark and dangerous, that made Clara's blood run cold.

"What are you doing?" Clara asked, her voice trembling, but trying to sound stronger than she felt.

Alex didn't answer. He just stood there, his eyes boring into hers, unblinking. Then, without a word, he turned and stepped outside, disappearing into the night.

Clara's legs felt like they were going to give out beneath her. She stumbled forward, catching herself on the edge of the counter. Emma was right behind her, her breathing fast and shallow.

"He's gone," Emma whispered, her voice filled with fear. "What do we do?"

Clara shook her head, her mind struggling to process what had just happened. "I... I don't know."

The wind howled outside, the cold air seeping into the kitchen. The door swung slightly on its hinges, the sound filling the room with an eerie creak. Clara stared at the open doorway, her heart pounding.

They were alone now. Alone in a dark, isolated inn, with a storm raging outside, and a man who had just disappeared into the night.

Clara's mind raced, her thoughts jumbled and chaotic. What was Alex doing? Why had he left? Where was he going? And more importantly, what was he planning?

As the questions swirled in her mind, Clara realized one thing with chilling clarity: They were no longer safe. Not here. Not in this inn. Not with Alex out there, somewhere in the darkness.

And they had no idea what he was going to do next.

6

Chapter 6

The wind howled through the trees, a mournful wail that seemed to echo the fear gripping everyone inside Snowridge Inn. The storm had picked up again, snow battering the windows as if trying to break through. Clara stood in the kitchen, her heart pounding in her chest, staring at the open door where Alex had disappeared into the night. She felt rooted to the spot, her mind reeling with questions, each more terrifying than the last.

"What do we do?" Emma's voice was a whisper, her eyes wide with panic.

Clara forced herself to move, to think. "We need to find Charles and Margaret," she said, her voice firmer than she felt. "We need to tell them what's happened."

Emma nodded, though she looked as though she might collapse at any moment. Clara took a deep breath, trying to steady herself. She had to stay calm, had to keep it together. If she lost it now, they were all in trouble.

Together, they hurried out of the kitchen, the hallway seeming darker and narrower than before. The flickering lights cast long shadows that danced on the walls, making everything feel more oppressive. Clara's pulse raced as they moved through the inn, her mind flashing back to Alex's cold, unblinking stare. What had he been planning? Why had he left?

They found Charles in the lounge, sitting by the fire with Margaret, both of them deep in conversation. The tension in the room was palpable, but it was nothing compared to the fear that gripped Clara as she approached them.

"Charles," Clara said, her voice trembling despite her efforts to stay calm. "We need to talk. Now."

Charles looked up, his brow furrowing as he took in Clara's and Emma's pale faces. "What's wrong?" he asked, his tone serious.

"Alex," Clara said, her voice barely above a whisper. "He's gone. We… we found the kitchen door open, and he just… walked out. Into the storm."

Margaret's hand flew to her mouth, her eyes wide with shock. "What? He left? Just like that?"

Clara nodded, her mind racing. "We have to figure out what he's planning. We need to search his room, see if he left anything behind."

Charles didn't hesitate. He stood up, his expression grim. "You're right. We need to know what he was doing here. If he left any clues, we have to find them."

Margaret hesitated, her face pale. "But what if he comes back?"

"We'll cross that bridge when we come to it," Charles said, his tone firm. "Right now, we need answers."

The group made their way to the second floor, the tension between them growing with every step. The inn was eerily quiet, the only sound the creaking of the floorboards under their feet. Clara's heart pounded in her chest as they reached Alex's door, the wood worn and scratched from years of use.

Charles took a deep breath, his hand hovering over the doorknob. "Are we ready?"

Clara and Margaret exchanged a nervous glance, but they both nodded. Charles turned the knob slowly, pushing the door open with a low creak. The room beyond was dark, the curtains drawn tightly shut. It smelled faintly of damp wool and something else—something metallic and sharp, like gun oil.

Clara felt a shiver run down her spine as they stepped inside. The room was neat, almost too neat. The bed was made with military precision, the corners tucked in tightly. There was a small duffel bag in the corner, the same bag Sarah and Daniel had mentioned. It looked innocent enough, but Clara's stomach twisted at the thought of what might be inside.

Margaret flipped the light switch, flooding the room with harsh, artificial light. The sudden brightness made Clara wince, but it also revealed the stark emptiness of the space. There was no sign of Alex's presence, no personal items, no indication that anyone had been staying here at all.

"Where do we start?" Emma asked, her voice trembling.

"The bag," Charles said, his tone decisive. "Let's see what he was carrying with him."

Clara moved toward the duffel bag, her heart pounding in her ears. She crouched down, her fingers trembling as she unzipped it. The sound of the zipper echoed in the silence, sharp and grating. Inside, she found clothes—simple, nondescript, the kind that could belong to anyone. But as she dug deeper, her fingers brushed against something cold and hard.

Her breath caught in her throat as she pulled out the object. It was a small handgun, just as Sarah and Daniel had said. The metal was cold and heavy in her hands, and it sent a shiver of fear through her.

"Careful," Charles warned, his voice low. "Don't touch the trigger."

Clara nodded, carefully setting the gun aside on the bed. The sight of it sent a jolt of adrenaline through her, the reality of the situation hitting her full force. This wasn't just some strange man staying at the inn. This was something far more dangerous, far more sinister.

Margaret crossed herself, her face pale. "What was he planning to do with that?"

"I don't know," Clara replied, her voice shaky. "But I don't think it was anything good."

Charles moved to the bed, picking up the gun and examining it closely. "It's loaded," he said, his voice grim. "And it's been used recently. There's residue in the barrel."

Clara's heart skipped a beat. "Used? But... on what?"

Charles didn't answer, his expression dark. He set the gun down carefully, as if it might go off at any moment, and turned back to the bag. "Let's see what else is in here."

They continued to search the bag, finding more clothes, a few toiletries, and a small black notebook. Clara opened it, her hands shaking slightly. The pages were filled with neat, precise handwriting, but the language was unfamiliar.

"What is this?" Clara asked, flipping through the pages.

"Let me see," Margaret said, reaching out for the notebook. She frowned as she examined the writing. "It's... code. Or some kind of shorthand. I can't make heads or tails of it."

Charles leaned over to take a look, his brow furrowing. "This isn't just a traveler's journal. This is something else entirely."

"What do we do with it?" Emma asked, her voice trembling. "We can't read it. We don't know what it says."

"We hold onto it," Charles said, his tone firm. "If he comes back, this might be the leverage we need."

Clara's mind raced as she continued to search the room, looking for anything that might give them answers. But the room was almost disturbingly clean, as if Alex had taken great care to leave no trace of himself behind.

"Check the drawers," Charles suggested, moving to the small desk in the corner. "See if he hid anything."

Clara nodded, opening the nightstand drawer first. It was empty, save for a single sheet of paper folded neatly in the middle. She pulled it out, her breath catching as she unfolded it. The paper was old, yellowed with age, and the edges were frayed. The handwriting was elegant, almost too perfect, and it sent a chill down Clara's spine.

"What is it?" Margaret asked, her voice tense.

Clara stared at the paper, her heart pounding. "It's… it's a letter. But it doesn't make any sense."

"Read it," Charles urged, his eyes fixed on the paper in her hands.

Clara swallowed hard, her voice trembling as she read aloud. "Dearest L—

The time has come. You know what must be done.

Do not hesitate.

Trust no one.

This is the only way.

Yours forever,

A."

The room fell silent as Clara finished reading, the weight of the words hanging heavily in the air. She stared at the letter, trying to make sense of it, but the more she thought about it, the more confused she became.

"Who's 'L'?" Emma asked, her voice barely above a whisper. "And who's 'A'?"

"I don't know," Clara admitted, her mind racing. "But this… this isn't just some random note. This is a message. A warning."

"But what does it mean?" Margaret asked, her voice filled with fear. "What's the 'only way'?"

Charles took the letter from Clara, his expression grave as he examined it. "This could be anything. A plan, a threat… we don't know. But whatever it is, it's important. And it's dangerous."

Clara felt a chill run down her spine, the reality of the situation settling over her like a heavy blanket. They were in way over their heads. Whatever Alex was involved in, it was far more dangerous than they'd imagined.

"We need to keep this safe," Charles said, folding the letter carefully and slipping it into his pocket. "Along with the notebook. If Alex comes back, we can't let him get his hands on these."

Margaret nodded, though her face was pale. "But what if he doesn't come back? What if he's… what if he's out there, planning something?"

"We don't have any answers yet," Charles said, his tone steady. "But we're going to find out. We'll figure this out, Margaret. We just have to stay calm."

Clara's mind was spinning, the fear and confusion threatening to overwhelm her. She felt like they were trapped in a nightmare, each new discovery pulling them deeper into the darkness. She couldn't shake the feeling that they were running out of time, that whatever Alex had been planning was about to unfold.

"What do we do now?" Emma asked, her voice trembling. "What if he comes back?"

Charles took a deep breath, his expression resolute. "We prepare. We stay vigilant. And we wait."

Clara's stomach twisted with dread at the thought of waiting, of doing nothing while the threat loomed over them. But she knew Charles was right. They had no choice but to bide their time, to stay on guard until they could figure out what Alex was after.

As they left the room, Clara couldn't shake the feeling that they were being watched, that Alex was somehow still there, lurking in the shadows, waiting for the right moment to strike. The inn felt colder, darker, the once cozy atmosphere now suffocating.

They reconvened in the lounge, the fire still burning low in the hearth. Margaret looked exhausted, her hands trembling as she poured herself a cup of tea. Emma sat beside her, her eyes red-rimmed with tears she was struggling to hold back.

Charles stood by the window, his expression thoughtful as he stared out into the storm. Clara joined him, the weight of the situation pressing down on her shoulders.

"What do you think he's doing out there?" Clara asked quietly.

Charles didn't answer right away, his gaze fixed on the swirling snow outside. Finally, he spoke, his tone heavy with concern. "Whatever it is, it can't be good."

Clara shivered, the chill from the window seeping into her bones. The darkness outside seemed to press in on the inn, the storm a relentless force that refused to let up. She felt trapped, like a caged animal, the walls of the inn closing in around her.

They spent the rest of the evening in a tense silence, each of them lost in their own thoughts. Every creak of the floorboards, every gust of wind against the windows sent a jolt of fear through Clara, her nerves stretched to the breaking point. She couldn't stop thinking about the gun, the letter, the notebook filled with coded writing. It was all too much, too overwhelming.

Finally, Margaret broke the silence, her voice shaky. "We need to get some rest. We can't do anything tonight. We'll be no good to each other if we're all exhausted."

Charles nodded, though his eyes remained on the window. "She's right. We need to sleep. We'll figure out our next steps in the morning."

Clara didn't know how she was supposed to sleep with everything that had happened, but she knew they didn't have much choice. They needed to be rested, alert. Whatever Alex was planning, they had to be ready.

They each returned to their rooms, the atmosphere heavy with fear and uncertainty. Clara felt like a prisoner in her own mind, the thoughts swirling endlessly, refusing to settle. She couldn't stop thinking about Alex, about the gun, about the cryptic letter. What did it all mean? And what were they supposed to do?

As she lay in bed, the darkness pressing in around her, Clara's thoughts raced. She couldn't shake the feeling that they were running out of time, that whatever was coming, it was inevitable. She could feel it, like a storm gathering on the horizon, the pressure building until it was ready to break.

But she also knew that she couldn't give in to the fear. She had to stay strong, had to be ready. They all did.

Clara closed her eyes, forcing herself to take slow, deep breaths. The wind howled outside, the snow battering the windows like a relentless force of nature. But inside, it was quiet, the only sound the faint crackling of the fire in the lounge below.

As she finally drifted off to sleep, her thoughts were filled with the images of Alex's cold, unblinking eyes, the weight of the gun in her hands, the cryptic message on the letter. They haunted her dreams, a constant reminder that the danger was far from over.

And in the darkness, something stirred. Something that had been waiting, watching, biding its time.

Because the storm was far from over, and the worst was yet to come.

7

Chapter 7

The night passed in fits and starts, Clara's sleep shattered by restless dreams and the ominous howl of the wind outside. The weight of the unknown pressed down on her, refusing to let her slip into the peaceful oblivion she so desperately needed. Every creak of the floorboards, every rustle of the wind seemed amplified in the silence of the inn, like whispers in the dark.

When she finally gave up on sleep, the room was still cloaked in darkness. The fire in the hearth had burned down to embers, casting a dim orange glow across the walls. Clara sat up, rubbing her eyes and glancing at the clock on the nightstand. It was just after five in the morning. Too early for most people to be awake, but Clara knew she wouldn't find any more rest tonight.

She threw off the covers and stood up, the cold air biting at her skin. She dressed quickly, pulling on a thick sweater and jeans, before grabbing her notebook. There was no point in staying in her room any longer. She needed to move, to do something, anything to keep her mind from spiraling further into anxiety.

The inn was eerily silent as she made her way downstairs, the old wooden steps creaking underfoot. The darkness was oppressive, wrapping around her like a heavy blanket, but she pushed through it, her mind focused on the task ahead. She needed answers, and she needed them now.

Clara found the lounge empty, the fire reduced to a few glowing embers in the hearth. She stared at the dying flames for a moment, the remnants of warmth doing little to chase away the chill that had settled deep in her bones. Then, with a sigh, she set her notebook on the coffee table and headed to the kitchen, hoping to find some coffee to help clear her head.

The kitchen was dark, the only light coming from the faint glow of the moon through the window. The wind had died down outside, leaving behind an eerie stillness that made Clara's skin prickle. She felt like she was the only person left in the world, the isolation of the inn pressing down on her.

She found the coffee pot and set it to brew, the familiar hum of the machine a small comfort in the silence. As the aroma of coffee filled the room, Clara leaned against the counter, her mind racing with everything that had happened. Alex's disappearance, the gun, the cryptic letter—it was all too much, too overwhelming. But she couldn't afford to let fear take over. She had to stay focused, had to figure out what was going on before it was too late.

The coffee finished brewing, and Clara poured herself a cup, cradling it in her hands as she made her way back to the lounge. The warmth of the mug seeped into her fingers, but it did little to ease the chill that had settled in her chest.

She was halfway across the room when she heard it—a soft creak, barely audible over the sound of her own footsteps.

Clara froze, her heart skipping a beat. She listened, straining to hear anything over the pounding of her pulse.

There it was again. A faint rustling, like fabric brushing against wood. The sound was coming from the hallway, just outside the lounge. Clara's breath caught in her throat, her mind racing. Who could it be? Was it Alex? Had he returned?

She set her coffee down on the table, her hands trembling. She couldn't just stand there, frozen in fear. She had to find out what was going on.

Clara moved toward the hallway, her steps slow and cautious. The shadows seemed to close in around her, the darkness feeling thicker, more oppressive with each step. She reached the doorway and peered into the hall, her breath hitching as she saw a figure standing in the shadows.

For a moment, panic gripped her. But then the figure stepped into the faint light from the lounge, and Clara let out a shaky breath. It wasn't Alex. It was Charles.

He looked as startled as she felt, his expression a mix of relief and concern. "Clara," he said, his voice low. "You're up early."

Clara managed a small smile, though her heart was still pounding. "I couldn't sleep. Too much on my mind."

Charles nodded, his gaze drifting down the hallway as if he was expecting something—or someone—to appear. "Same here. I thought I heard something, but… I guess it was just my imagination."

Clara frowned, glancing down the hallway herself. "Are you sure? With everything that's happened…"

Charles shook his head, though his eyes were still shadowed with worry. "I checked the doors and windows. Everything's locked up tight. I think it's just the wind playing tricks on us."

Clara wanted to believe him, but the unease gnawing at her

refused to let go. "Maybe we should check Alex's room again. Just to be sure."

Charles hesitated, his gaze lingering on the hallway before he finally nodded. "It can't hurt."

They made their way to the second floor, the oppressive silence of the inn weighing heavily on them. The hallway leading to the guest rooms was dark, the only light coming from the faint glow of the moon through the small windows. Clara's heart pounded in her chest as they approached Alex's door, the memory of their last search still fresh in her mind.

Charles reached for the doorknob, his hand steady despite the tension in the air. He turned it slowly, pushing the door open with a low creak. The room beyond was just as they'd left it—dark, empty, and unnervingly neat. The bed was still made, the duffel bag still lying open in the corner.

"Nothing's changed," Charles murmured, his voice barely above a whisper.

Clara nodded, though her eyes were drawn to the window at the far end of the room. The curtains were still drawn tightly shut, blocking out the moonlight. But there was something about them that caught her attention, something that didn't feel right.

"Charles," she said quietly, nodding toward the window. "Look at the curtains."

Charles followed her gaze, his brow furrowing. "What about them?"

"They're… moving," Clara whispered, her pulse quickening. "Like there's a draft."

Charles frowned, stepping closer to the window. He reached out and pulled the curtains aside, revealing the window behind them. It was closed, but as Clara stepped closer, she saw what had caught her attention. There was a faint gap between the window and the frame, just wide enough for a thin sliver of air to seep through.

"It's not sealed properly," Charles muttered, running his fingers along the gap. "That's what's causing the movement."

Clara's mind raced as she stared at the window. "But why is it like that? Why wasn't it closed all the way?"

Charles turned to look at her, his expression darkening. "Maybe because someone didn't want it to be."

Clara's breath caught in her throat. "You think… you think Alex used this window to get out?"

"It's possible," Charles said grimly. "It would explain how he disappeared so easily. He might have slipped out before we even realized he was gone."

Clara's mind raced, trying to piece together what it all meant. "But why? Why would he sneak out like that? What was he planning?"

Charles didn't answer, his eyes fixed on the window as if it held the answers they were looking for. Finally, he turned away, his expression grim. "We need to tell Margaret."

They made their way back downstairs, the weight of the discovery pressing down on them. Clara's thoughts were spinning, the fear and confusion swirling together in a dizzying whirlwind. What was Alex up to? Why had he left? And, more importantly, what was he planning to do next?

They found Margaret in the kitchen, preparing breakfast. She looked up as they entered, her expression tight with worry. "What is it?" she asked, her voice filled with tension. "Did something happen?"

Charles explained quickly, keeping his voice low. He told her about the window, the draft, and their suspicion that Alex had used it to slip out unnoticed. By the time he finished, Margaret's face had gone pale, her hands trembling slightly.

"He could be anywhere," she whispered, her voice trembling. "What do we do? How do we protect ourselves?"

Charles placed a reassuring hand on her shoulder, his tone steady. "We stay vigilant. We don't let our guard down. And we keep an eye on each other. We can't let fear take over."

Margaret nodded, though the fear in her eyes was unmistakable. "I'll make sure all the doors and windows are secure. We can't afford to take any chances."

Clara's heart ached for Margaret. She had been so strong, so determined to keep everyone safe, but now she looked as though the weight of it all was finally catching up to her. Clara wanted to offer some words of comfort, something to ease the burden, but the truth was, she didn't know what to say. They were all in the dark, stumbling through the unknown, and the fear was like a living thing, growing stronger with every passing minute.

As Margaret went to check the doors and windows, Clara and Charles sat down at the kitchen table, the silence between them heavy with unspoken fears. Clara wrapped her hands around her coffee cup, the warmth doing little to chase away the chill that had settled deep in her bones.

"What if he doesn't come back?" Clara asked quietly, her voice barely above a whisper. "What if he's out there, planning something? Something terrible?"

Charles didn't answer right away, his eyes focused on the steam rising from his coffee. Finally, he spoke, his voice heavy with concern. "We have to prepare for that possibility. We can't let our guard down. Not for a second."

Clara nodded, though the thought of living in constant fear

made her stomach twist. "And if he does come back?"

"Then we deal with him," Charles said firmly. "We can't let him hurt anyone. Whatever it takes, we stop him."

The resolve in his voice gave Clara some comfort, but the fear still gnawed at her, a constant, nagging worry that refused to be silenced. She couldn't stop thinking about the gun, the letter, the coded notebook. What if they had missed something? What if there was more to the puzzle than they had realized?

"I'm going to take another look around," Clara said, standing up. "There has to be something we're missing."

Charles nodded, though his expression was still tense. "Be careful, Clara. Don't take any unnecessary risks."

Clara offered him a small, reassuring smile, though her heart was pounding in her chest. "I will."

She left the kitchen and made her way back upstairs, her mind racing. She had to find something, anything that would give them a clue about what Alex was planning. She couldn't just sit around and wait for the worst to happen.

She started with the hallway, checking the doors and windows, looking for anything out of place. But everything seemed normal, too normal. It was as if Alex had taken great care to leave no trace of himself behind.

Frustration gnawed at her as she moved from room to room, her search turning up nothing but more questions. How had Alex managed to disappear so easily? What was he planning? And why did she feel like they were all being played, like pieces on a chessboard?

Finally, she returned to Alex's room, her heart pounding as she stepped inside. The room was just as they had left it, dark and empty, with the faint draft from the window still stirring the curtains. Clara's eyes were drawn to the duffel bag in the corner, the contents still scattered across the floor from their earlier search.

There had to be something they had missed. Something hidden, something small but important. Clara knelt beside the bag, her fingers trembling as she began to search through it again. She dug through the clothes, the toiletries, the empty pockets, looking for anything out of the ordinary.

And then she found it.

It was a small, folded piece of paper, tucked into the lining of the bag. It was so well-hidden that Clara had almost missed it, but the corner had been sticking out just enough for her to catch a glimpse of it.

Her heart skipped a beat as she pulled the paper out, unfolding it carefully. The handwriting was the same as the letter they had found earlier—elegant, precise, and almost too perfect. But this time, the message was different. This time, it was a set of coordinates.

Clara's breath caught in her throat as she stared at the numbers, her mind racing. Coordinates. Why would Alex have a set of coordinates hidden in his bag? What were they for?

She stood up quickly, the paper clutched tightly in her hand. She had to show this to Charles. They needed to figure out where these coordinates led, and fast.

Clara hurried downstairs, her pulse quickening with every step. When she reached the kitchen, she found Charles and Margaret deep in conversation, their expressions serious.

"Charles," Clara said, her voice breathless. "I found something. In Alex's bag."

Charles looked up, his brow furrowing in concern. "What is it?"

Clara handed him the piece of paper, her heart pounding as she watched him unfold it. "It's a set of coordinates. I don't know what they mean, but… it has to be important."

Charles's eyes scanned the paper, his expression darkening. "Coordinates? Why would he have these?"

"I don't know," Clara admitted, her mind racing. "But we need to find out where they lead."

Margaret, who had been listening quietly, looked up, her eyes wide with fear. "You don't think… you don't think he's planning something, do you?"

Charles didn't answer right away, his gaze fixed on the numbers on the paper. Finally, he spoke, his voice grim. "We can't rule anything out. We need to figure out where these coordinates lead, and we need to do it now."

Clara nodded, her resolve strengthening. They were getting closer to the truth, closer to uncovering whatever Alex was hiding. But the fear gnawed at her, a constant reminder that they were running out of time.

"Do you have a map?" Clara asked, her voice trembling slightly.

Margaret nodded, standing up quickly. "I think there's one in the office. I'll go get it."

As Margaret left the kitchen, Clara and Charles exchanged a tense glance. The weight of the situation pressed down on them, the fear and uncertainty thickening the air around them. They were so close to finding the answers they needed, but the danger was growing with every passing second.

Margaret returned with the map, spreading it out on the kitchen table. Charles examined the coordinates again, his expression serious as he searched for the corresponding location on the map. Clara watched anxiously, her heart pounding in her chest.

Finally, Charles's finger stopped on a spot near the edge of the map. "Here," he said, his voice tight. "The coordinates lead here. It's not far from the inn."

Clara leaned in, her eyes scanning the map. The spot Charles had pointed to was deep in the forest, miles from the nearest road. It was isolated, hidden away from the rest of the world.

"Why would he go there?" Clara asked, her voice trembling. "What's out there?"

Charles shook his head, his expression grim. "I don't know. But whatever it is, it's important to him. And that means it's important to us."

Margaret looked up, her face pale. "Are you… are you planning to go out there? To those coordinates?"

"We have to," Charles said, his tone firm. "We need to know what he's hiding. We can't just sit here and wait for him to make the first move."

Clara's mind raced, the fear gnawing at her. The thought of venturing out into the forest, especially with the storm still raging, was terrifying. But they had no choice. They needed answers, and this was their only lead.

"I'm coming with you," Clara said, her voice steady despite the fear in her chest.

Charles looked at her, his eyes filled with concern. "Clara, you don't have to—"

"Yes, I do," Clara interrupted, her voice firm. "We're in this together, Charles. I'm not going to sit back and do nothing while you take all the risks."

Charles hesitated, his gaze searching hers. Finally, he nodded, his expression resolute. "All right. But we have to be careful. We don't know what we're walking into."

Margaret's voice trembled as she spoke. "Please, be safe. And if… if something goes wrong…"

"We'll be careful," Charles assured her, his tone gentle. "But we have to do this."

Clara's heart pounded as they made their final preparations, gathering supplies and bundling up against the cold. The fear eating at her, but she pushed it down, focusing on the task ahead. They were close—so close to uncovering the truth. But the danger was growing with every step they took.

As they stepped outside into the biting cold, Clara couldn't shake the feeling that they were being watched, that Alex was out there, somewhere in the darkness, waiting for them. The snow crunched underfoot as they made their way into the forest, the darkness pressing in around them.

Clara's breath came in short, sharp gasps, her pulse racing as they moved deeper into the woods. The wind howled through the trees, sending shivers down her spine. But she pushed on, her resolve strengthening with every step.

They reached the coordinates just as dawn began to break, the faint light of the rising sun casting long shadows across the snow. The spot was isolated, hidden away from the rest of the world, just as Clara had feared.

But what they found there was beyond anything she could have imagined.

As they stepped into the clearing, Clara's breath caught in her throat. In the center of the clearing was a small, makeshift camp. A tent, half-buried in the snow, and a small fire pit, long since extinguished. But that wasn't what stopped Clara in her tracks.

It was the figure lying in the snow, motionless, half-covered by the drifts.

Charles reached the figure first, his expression darkening as he knelt beside it. Clara's heart pounded in her chest as she joined him, her breath catching in her throat.

The figure was Alex.

He was lying on his back, his face pale and lifeless, his eyes staring up at the sky. The snow around him was stained with blood, the crimson stark against the white.

Clara's mind raced, her thoughts jumbled and chaotic. "Is he…?"

Charles nodded grimly, his fingers checking for a pulse that wasn't there. "He's gone."

Clara's breath hitched, the reality of the situation hitting her like a physical blow. Alex was dead. Whatever he had been planning, whatever secrets he had been hiding, they had died with him.

But the fear haunted her, a constant reminder that this wasn't over. Alex had been hiding something—something important, something dangerous. And now, they were left to pick up the pieces.

Clara's gaze drifted to the tent, her heart pounding in her chest. Whatever Alex had been hiding, it was in there. And they had to find it.

With trembling hands, Clara reached for the tent flap, pulling it open slowly. The cold air rushed in, sending a shiver down her spine. But what she found inside was more chilling than the cold.

A small, metal box, half-buried in the snow. It was locked, the metal cold and unforgiving against Clara's fingers. But it was the key to everything. The answers they had been searching for.

Charles reached for the box, his expression grim. "We need

to get this back to the inn. We'll figure out how to open it there."

Clara nodded, her mind racing with questions, fears, and the sickening realization that they had only just begun to unravel the mystery. And the truth, whatever it was, would be far more dangerous than they could have ever imagined.

8

Chapter 8

The hike back to Snowridge Inn was a blur, the cold biting at Clara's cheeks and stinging her eyes. The weight of the small metal box in Charles's hands seemed to grow heavier with each step, its secrets pressing down on them like a physical burden. The snow crunched underfoot, muffling their movements, but nothing could silence the thoughts racing through Clara's mind.

Alex was dead.

The image of his lifeless body lying in the snow was burned into her memory, the sight of the blood stark against the pristine white. What had happened to him? How had he died? And more importantly, what had he been hiding in that box?

The questions swirled in Clara's mind, but the answers felt just out of reach, like trying to grasp at smoke. The box was their only clue, their only chance at understanding what Alex had been involved in. But what if they couldn't open it? What if the answers were locked away forever?

Clara shook her head, trying to clear the fog of fear and doubt that threatened to overwhelm her. She had to stay focused, had to keep her mind sharp. There was no room for hesitation now. They were on the brink of something big, something dangerous, and they couldn't afford to lose their nerve.

The inn came into view through the trees, its dark silhouette standing out against the snow-covered landscape. The storm had subsided, leaving behind a blanket of white that seemed to glow in the early morning light. The sight of the inn, usually so welcoming, now filled Clara with a sense of foreboding. The walls that had once felt like a refuge now felt like a prison, closing in around them with each passing moment.

As they approached the inn, Clara glanced over at Charles. His face was set in a grim line, his eyes focused on the box in his hands. She could see the tension in his posture, the worry etched into his features. He was trying to stay strong, for all of them, but Clara could tell that the weight of the situation was getting to him too.

They entered the inn through the back door, the warmth of the kitchen a stark contrast to the biting cold outside. Margaret was there, pacing back and forth, her hands wringing together in nervousness. She looked up as they entered, her eyes wide with worry.

"Did you find anything?" she asked, her voice trembling.

Charles held up the box, his expression serious. "We found this. It was in the tent where Alex… where we found him. He's deceased."

Margaret's eyes widened as she took in the sight of the box. "What's in it?"

"We don't know," Charles admitted, his tone heavy with frustration. "It's locked. But whatever's inside, it's important. I can feel it."

Margaret nodded, her face pale. "What do we do now?"

"We need to figure out how to open it," Clara said, her voice firmer than she felt. "There has to be a way."

Charles set the box down on the kitchen table, his eyes scanning it for any sign of a keyhole or latch. But the box was smooth, the metal cool and unyielding, with no visible way to open it.

"It's like it's sealed shut," Charles muttered, running his fingers along the edges. "No seams, no hinges… nothing."

Clara frowned, her mind racing. "Maybe there's a hidden mechanism? Something we're not seeing?"

"Could be," Charles agreed, though his tone was laced with doubt. "But without knowing what it is, we're just guessing."

Margaret looked between them, her worry deepening. "What if… what if we can't open it? What if the answers we need are locked inside forever?"

Clara's stomach twisted at the thought. The idea that they might never know what Alex had been hiding, that the truth could be just out of reach, was almost too much to bear. But she couldn't give in to despair. They had to keep trying, had to find a way.

"There has to be something," Clara said, more to herself than to the others. "We just have to think."

Charles nodded, though his expression remained grim. "Maybe there's something in Alex's other belongings. Something we missed."

Margaret's eyes flickered with hope. "You think there could be a key? Or a code?"

"Possibly," Charles said, though his tone was cautious. "It's worth checking."

Clara nodded, her mind already working through the possibilities. The notebook, the letter... there had to be a clue somewhere, something they hadn't noticed before. They couldn't afford to overlook anything now.

Margaret led them to the lounge, where they spread out Alex's belongings on the coffee table. The notebook, the letter, and the few personal items they had found in his duffel bag. Margaret had placed the gun in the kitchen, locking it away in a drawer for safekeeping. Clara's eyes lingered on the gun, a shiver running down her spine at the thought of what might have happened if Alex had used it.

"We should start with the notebook," Clara suggested, her voice steady. "There might be a code or something in there that can help us open the box."

Charles picked up the notebook, his brow furrowing as he flipped through the pages. "It's all in code. But maybe if we compare it to the letter, we can find a pattern."

Margaret handed him the letter, her hands trembling slightly. "Do you think Alex wrote this? Or... or someone else?"

Clara frowned, her mind racing. "It's possible he wrote it himself. But the handwriting is so precise, so elegant... it doesn't match what we've seen of him."

"Maybe it's someone else's handwriting," Charles suggested, his eyes scanning the letter. "Someone he was working with."

Margaret's face paled at the thought. "You think there's someone else out there? Someone who might come looking for this box?"

Clara didn't want to consider the possibility, but the horror she felt ate away at her. If Alex had been working with someone, and that person was still out there... they could be in even more danger than they realized.

"We need to focus on the box," Charles said, his tone firm.

"If we can open it, we might find the answers we need."

They spent the next hour poring over the notebook and the letter, searching for any hint of a code or pattern that could help them unlock the box. The tension in the room was palpable, each of them acutely aware of the stakes. Every minute that passed felt like an eternity, the pressure mounting with each failed attempt.

"This isn't getting us anywhere," Charles muttered, frustration evident in his voice. "We're missing something. There has to be a connection, but we're not seeing it."

Clara's eyes ached from staring at the tiny, precise handwriting, the code like a puzzle she couldn't solve. She leaned back in her chair, rubbing her temples as she tried to think. There had to be something they were overlooking, something small but crucial.

Then, something clicked in her mind.

"Wait," Clara said, her voice sharper than she intended. "What if it's not just a code? What if it's a combination?"

Charles looked up, his brow furrowed. "What do you mean?"

Clara's mind raced as she tried to piece it together. "Look at the way the numbers are arranged in the notebook. They're grouped together, like they're part of a sequence. And the letter... it's almost like a set of instructions."

Charles's eyes widened as he considered her words. "You think the code in the notebook is a combination for the box?"

"It's possible," Clara said, her heart pounding. "We've been looking at it like a puzzle, but what if it's a lock? If we can figure out the right combination, we might be able to open the box."

Margaret's eyes lit up with hope. "But how do we figure out the combination? The numbers in the notebook don't seem to follow any pattern."

Clara chewed her lip, her mind racing. "Maybe it's not about the numbers themselves, but the way they're arranged. Like… like a sequence we have to follow."

Charles nodded, his eyes scanning the notebook with renewed focus. "We'll need to be careful. If this is a combination lock, one wrong move could jam it shut."

The tension in the room thickened as they worked together, carefully studying the numbers in the notebook, comparing them to the letter, and trying to discern the correct sequence. Every now and then, one of them would suggest a possibility, only to be met with frustrated silence when it didn't work.

Clara's nerves were frayed, her patience wearing thin. But she couldn't give up now. They were so close, and the thought of leaving the box unopened, of never knowing what Alex had been hiding, was unbearable.

Finally, after what felt like hours, Charles set down the notebook with a heavy sigh. "I think we have it."

Clara's heart skipped a beat. "You do?"

Charles nodded, though his expression was serious. "It's a sequence, like you said. But it's more complicated than I expected. The numbers in the notebook correspond to the letters in the letter. It's like a cipher, but with a twist."

Clara frowned, trying to follow his explanation. "So how do we open the box?"

Charles took a deep breath, his hands steady as he reached for the box. "I think we have to enter the sequence on the box itself. There are no visible buttons or dials, but if we press the right spots in the right order…"

Clara watched in tense silence as Charles carefully examined the box, his fingers tracing the smooth surface. It seemed impossible that the metal could hide any kind of mechanism, but she trusted Charles's judgment. He was meticulous, cautious, and if anyone could figure it out, it was him.

He pressed his fingers against the side of the box, applying pressure to a spot that seemed no different from the rest. Nothing happened. He tried another spot, then another, following the sequence they had painstakingly deciphered.

The room was silent, the tension thick enough to cut with a knife. Clara held her breath, her heart pounding as she watched Charles work. The box remained stubbornly closed, each failed attempt sending a wave of frustration and fear through her.

But then, just as Clara was beginning to lose hope, there was a faint click.

The sound was so soft that Clara almost didn't hear it, but Charles's eyes widened in triumph. He pressed another spot on the box, and there was another click, slightly louder this time. Clara's pulse quickened, her eyes locked on the box as it began to shift, the metal seams separating ever so slightly.

"It's working," Charles whispered, his voice filled with a mixture of awe and relief.

Clara leaned in closer, her breath catching in her throat as the box slowly, almost reluctantly, began to open. The metal plates slid apart with a soft hiss, revealing a small, velvet-lined compartment within.

For a moment, no one moved. The room was so still, so silent, that Clara could hear the faint rustle of the curtains as the wind picked up outside. Her heart pounded in her ears, her mind racing with anticipation and dread. Whatever was inside that box was the key to everything, and she wasn't sure she was ready to see it.

Charles reached into the box, his hand trembling slightly as he pulled out a small, folded piece of paper. It was old, yellowed with age, the edges frayed and delicate. He unfolded it carefully, his eyes scanning the contents.

"What does it say?" Clara asked, her voice barely above a whisper.

Charles's eyes darkened as he read the paper, his expression growing more serious with each word. Finally, he looked up, his face pale.

"It's a list," he said quietly. "A list of names."

Clara's heart skipped a beat. "Names? What kind of names?"

Charles handed her the paper, his eyes filled with concern. "I don't know. But they're all crossed out."

Clara's hands trembled as she took the paper, her eyes scanning the list. The names were written in neat, precise handwriting, each one carefully crossed out with a thin line of ink. The sight of it sent a shiver down her spine, the reality of the situation settling over her like a heavy blanket.

"These people... they're dead," Clara whispered, her voice trembling. "This is... this is a hit list."

Margaret gasped, her hands flying to her mouth. "A hit list? But... but why? Why would Alex have something like this?"

Clara's mind raced, the fear gnawing at her. "I don't know. But this... this is what he was hiding. This is what he was involved in."

Charles's expression was grim. "Whoever these people were, they were targets. And Alex was either involved in their deaths or was trying to stop them."

Clara's heart pounded as she stared at the list, the names blurring together as her mind tried to process what she was seeing. This was beyond anything she could have imagined, a nightmare come to life. And now, they were caught in the middle of it.

"We need to take this to the authorities," Charles said, his voice firm. "This isn't something we can handle on our own."

Clara nodded, though the fear still gnawed at her. "But what if Alex's partner comes after us? What if they know we have this?"

Charles's expression darkened. "Then we need to be ready."

Margaret's face was pale, her hands trembling as she stared at the list. "What if... what if we're on that list?"

Clara's breath caught in her throat at the thought. The idea that they could be targets, that their lives could be in danger, was almost too much to bear. But she couldn't let the fear paralyze her. They had to stay strong, had to see this through.

"We'll figure this out," Charles said, his voice filled with resolve. "We'll find out who's behind this and why. And we'll make sure they can't hurt anyone else."

Clara nodded, though her heart was still pounding in her chest. The fear was a constant, gnawing presence, but she knew they couldn't let it consume them. They had to stay focused, had to keep moving forward.

As they sat together in the lounge, the list of names spread out on the table between them, Clara couldn't shake the feeling that they were standing on the edge of a precipice, one wrong move away from falling into the abyss. The storm outside had subsided, but the storm within was just beginning to brew.

The truth, whatever it was, was more dangerous than they had ever imagined. And the worst was yet to come.

9

Chapter 9

The air inside the inn was thick with tension, the silence between them punctuated only by the occasional creak of the old wooden floorboards. Clara's heart pounded as she stared at the list of names, each one meticulously crossed out, a grim reminder of the danger that now loomed over them all. The revelation that they were entangled in something far more sinister than they could have imagined weighed heavily on her, making it difficult to think clearly.

Charles stood by the window, his brow furrowed in concentration as he looked out at the snow-covered landscape. The storm had finally passed, leaving behind a deep, pristine blanket of white that seemed to glow in the pale morning light. But the beauty of the scene did nothing to ease the dread that hung over them like a dark cloud.

"We need to get out of here," Clara said, breaking the oppressive silence. Her voice was steady, but her heart was racing. "We can't stay in this inn, not with everything we've found. We need to find help."

Charles nodded, his gaze still fixed on the snow outside. "I agree. But we have to be careful. Whoever is behind this, they're not going to let us just walk away."

Margaret sat in a chair by the fire, her hands clasped tightly in her lap. She looked pale and drawn, the fear etched into her features. "But how are we supposed to leave?" she asked, her voice trembling. "We're miles from the nearest town, and the roads are covered in snow. Even if we tried to drive out of here, we might not make it."

Clara felt a pang of frustration. She knew Margaret was right, but the thought of staying in the inn, vulnerable and exposed, was unbearable. They were sitting ducks, waiting for whatever—or whoever—might come for them next.

Just then, Emma, Sarah, and Daniel appeared in the doorway, their faces filled with a mixture of fear and confusion. They had been holed up in their rooms since the discovery of the list, and it was clear that the tension was getting to them as well.

"What's going on?" Daniel asked, his voice tense. "Why haven't we left yet?"

As Clara filled them in on the status of the roads, she saw the color drain from Emma's face. Sarah's expression hardened, and Daniel's jaw tightened. The reality of the situation was sinking in, and it was clear they were all feeling the same sense of dread.

"So we're just supposed to sit here and wait to be picked off one by one?" Sarah asked, her voice sharp with fear. "That's insane."

"We can't stay here," Daniel added, his tone filled with urgency. "We need to get out of here, now."

"I agree," Clara said, her voice firm. "But we need to be smart about this. We can't just run out into the snow and hope for the best. We need a plan."

Charles finally turned away from the window, his expression grim. "We should check the vehicles, see if we can get them started. If the roads are passable, we might be able to make it to the nearest town."

Clara nodded, feeling a glimmer of hope. "Okay. Let's do it."

They quickly bundled up in their coats, scarves, and gloves, the cold air seeping through the walls of the inn as they prepared to step outside. The tension in the group was discernable, each of them acutely aware of the danger they were in.

As they made their way to the back door, Clara couldn't shake the feeling that they were being watched, that someone—or something—was out there, waiting for them. The thought sent a shiver down her spine, but she pushed it aside, focusing on the task at hand.

They stepped out into the snow, the cold air biting at their skin. The landscape was eerily quiet, the only sound the crunch of their boots on the snow as they made their way toward the vehicles parked in the lot behind the inn.

Clara's breath hitched in her throat when she saw the cars. Something was wrong.

"Stop," she said, her voice barely above a whisper. "Look."

The group halted in their tracks, their eyes following Clara's gaze to the vehicles. At first, it wasn't immediately obvious what was wrong, but as they got closer, the reality of the situation hit them like a punch to the gut.

All of the tires were flat.

Someone had slashed them, leaving deep gashes in the rubber. The snow around the vehicles was stained with dark streaks where the tires had bled out their air.

"No," Emma whispered, her voice trembling with fear. "No, no, no…"

Sarah clenched her fists, her face contorted with anger. "Who did this? Who the hell did this?"

Charles moved closer to the vehicles, examining the damage. His expression was grim as he straightened up, his breath visible in the cold air. "This wasn't an accident. Someone did this deliberately. They wanted to make sure we couldn't leave."

Clara's heart raced as she tried to process the implications. Whoever had done this was still out there, watching them, waiting for the right moment to strike. They were trapped, isolated in the middle of nowhere, with no way to call for help and no way to escape.

"What do we do now?" Daniel asked, his voice filled with a mixture of fear and frustration. "We're stuck here."

"We have to go back inside," Charles said firmly. "We need to regroup, figure out our next move."

Clara felt a surge of frustration and fear, but she knew Charles was right. There was nothing they could do out here in the snow, and staying outside made them vulnerable. They had to get back to the relative safety of the inn and come up with a plan.

The group made their way back inside, the atmosphere tense and filled with a sense of impending doom. Clara's mind raced as she tried to think of a solution, but every idea seemed to lead to a dead end. Without their vehicles, they were trapped. The nearest town was miles away, and trekking through the snow on foot was too dangerous to even consider.

Once inside, they gathered in the lounge, the fire in the hearth doing little to chase away the chill that had settled in their bones. The sense of safety that the inn had once provided was gone, replaced by an agonizing sense of dread that refused to let go.

"What are we going to do?" Emma asked, her voice trembling. "We're trapped here. We can't leave, we can't call for help… what if whoever did this comes for us next?"

"We need to secure the inn," Charles said, his tone steady despite the fear in his eyes. "Make sure all the doors and windows are locked. We can't let anyone get inside."

"But what if they're already inside?" Sarah asked, her voice sharp with fear. "What if they're already here, watching us?"

Clara's blood ran cold at the thought. The idea that someone could be inside the inn, hiding in the shadows, waiting to strike, was almost too terrifying to comprehend. But they couldn't afford to ignore the possibility.

"We need to search the inn," Clara said, her voice firm. "Check every room, every corner."

Charles nodded, his expression serious. "Agreed. We'll split up into pairs. Clara, you go with Margaret. I'll take the ground floor with Daniel. Sarah, you and Emma take the upper floor."

The group exchanged tense glances, but no one argued. They were all too aware of the danger they were in, and the urgency of the situation left no room for hesitation.

As they prepared to search the inn, Clara felt a knot of anxiety tighten in her chest. The fear of what they might find—or who they might find—was almost suffocating. But she pushed it down, focusing on the task ahead.

Clara and Margaret started their search in the kitchen, checking the pantry, cupboards, and storage rooms. Everything seemed normal, but Clara couldn't shake the feeling that someone was lurking just out of sight.

Margaret was silent as they moved through the rooms, her hands trembling slightly as she opened doors and peered into dark corners. Clara could see the fear in her eyes, the way she kept glancing over her shoulder as if expecting something—or someone—to jump out at them.

The fear gnawed at Clara too, but she forced herself to stay calm, to keep moving. They had to be thorough, had to make sure they weren't missing anything.

When they finished checking the kitchen, they moved on to the dining room, then the lounge. The tension in the air was thick, every creak of the floorboards and rustle of the wind outside making Clara's heart race. But they found nothing out of the ordinary, no signs of an intruder.

They met up with Charles and Daniel in the hallway, both men looking equally tense. "Anything?" Charles asked, his voice low.

Clara shook her head. "Nothing. Everything seems normal."

Daniel frowned, his jaw clenched. "Same here. We checked every room, but there's no sign of anyone."

"Let's see how Sarah and Emma are doing," Charles suggested, his tone filled with concern. "Maybe they found something."

The group made their way upstairs, the old wooden steps creaking under their weight. The upper floor was dimly lit, the shadows long and deep as they approached the hallway where the guest rooms were located.

"Sarah? Emma?" Charles called out, his voice echoing slightly in the narrow corridor.

There was no response.

Clara's heart skipped a beat, the silence pressing in on her like a vice. She exchanged a worried glance with Charles before they continued down the hallway, their footsteps muffled on the thick carpet.

When they reached the end of the hallway, they found Sarah and Emma standing outside one of the guest rooms, their faces pale and tense. Emma's hands were clasped together, her knuckles white with fear, while Sarah's expression was a mixture of anger and anxiety.

"What's going on?" Charles asked, his voice filled with concern.

Sarah glanced at him, her eyes dark with worry. "We found something."

Clara's heart pounded in her chest as she stepped closer, her gaze following Sarah's to the door of the guest room. The door was slightly ajar, and as Clara peered inside, she felt a cold shiver run down her spine.

The room was a mess. The bed was unmade, the sheets tangled and thrown to the floor. The furniture had been overturned, drawers pulled out and their contents scattered across the room. The window was open, letting in the cold night air.

"What happened here?" Clara whispered, her voice trembling.

Emma shook her head, her eyes wide with fear. "We don't know. We found it like this."

Charles frowned, his expression serious as he stepped into the room, carefully avoiding the debris on the floor. "Whoever did this was looking for something."

"But what?" Clara asked, her mind racing. "What were they looking for?"

"Maybe it wasn't something they were looking for," Sarah suggested, her voice filled with unease. "Maybe it was someone."

Clara's blood ran cold at the thought. The idea that someone had been in this room, searching for one of them, sent a wave of fear crashing over her. But she couldn't let herself be paralyzed by it. They had to stay focused, had to figure out what was going on before it was too late.

"We need to stay together," Charles said firmly, his gaze sweeping over the room. "We can't split up again. Whoever did this might still be in the inn."

Clara nodded, her heart pounding. "We'll need to search the rest of the inn, but we have to be careful. If they're still here, we don't want to walk into a trap."

The group moved cautiously through the inn, checking every room, every corner, but there was no sign of the intruder. Whoever had trashed the guest room had disappeared, leaving behind only the chilling evidence of their presence.

By the time they finished searching, the fear had settled deep in Clara's bones, a constant, growing presence that refused to let go. They were trapped in the inn, isolated and vulnerable, with no way to call for help and no way to escape. And somewhere out there—whether inside the inn or lurking in the woods—someone was watching them, waiting for the right moment to strike.

As they gathered in the lounge once more, Clara couldn't shake the feeling that they were being toyed with, like pieces on a chessboard being moved into place for a final, deadly game. The thought sent a shiver down her spine, but she pushed it aside, focusing on the task at hand.

"We need to come up with a plan," Charles said, his voice steady despite the tension in the room. "We can't just sit here and wait for whoever did this to make their next move."

"But what can we do?" Margaret asked, her voice filled with fear. "We can't leave, we can't call for help… what options do we have?"

Clara's mind raced as she tried to think of a solution. "We need to secure the inn, make sure no one can get in—or out—without us knowing. We should block the doors and windows, make it as difficult as possible for anyone to enter."

Charles nodded in agreement. "And we should set up watches. We'll take turns keeping an eye on things, making sure no one sneaks up on us."

"I'll take the first watch," Daniel offered, his voice determined. "I'm not going to let whoever did this get the drop on us."

"I'll join you," Sarah said, her tone firm. "We'll cover more ground if there are two of us."

Clara felt a surge of gratitude for their willingness to step up, but the fear still gnawed at her. They were in uncharted territory, facing an enemy they couldn't see, and the stakes had never been higher.

As they moved to secure the inn, blocking the doors with furniture and covering the windows, Clara couldn't shake the feeling that they were sealing themselves inside a tomb. The inn, once a place of warmth and safety, now felt like a trap, the walls closing in around them with each passing moment.

When the preparations were finally complete, Clara found herself standing by the fire, staring into the flickering flames as her mind raced. The fear was a constant presence, but beneath it was a growing determination. They had to survive this. They had to find a way out.

Charles approached her, his expression serious but calm. "We'll get through this, Clara. We just have to stay focused."

Clara nodded, though the fear still lingered in the back of her mind. "I know. But whoever did this… they're not going to stop. They want something, and they're not going to let us go until they get it."

"Then we'll make sure they don't get it," Charles said firmly. "We'll fight back, whatever it takes."

Clara looked into his eyes, seeing the resolve there, and felt a spark of hope. They were in this together, and as long as they stood united, they had a chance.

As the night deepened and the shadows grew longer, Clara knew they were in for a fight. The storm outside had passed, but the storm within the inn was just beginning to brew. The tension in the air was thick, the fear almost palpable, but Clara refused to let it consume her.

They would survive this. They had to. And whatever secrets the inn held, whatever dangers awaited them, they would face it head-on, together.

10

Chapter 10

The night dragged on with an eerie stillness, the quiet so profound that every creak and whisper in the old inn seemed magnified. Clara sat by the fireplace, the flickering flames casting long shadows that danced on the walls, adding to the growing sense of unease that clung to her like a shroud. The room was warm, but the chill in her bones refused to dissipate. The events of the past hours played over and over in her mind, a loop of fear and confusion that she couldn't escape.

Charles sat across from her, his eyes sharp and alert despite the late hour. His gaze occasionally flicked toward the blocked windows and doors, as if expecting something—or someone—to break through at any moment. Margaret was curled up on one of the sofas, her eyes closed, though Clara doubted she was actually sleeping. The tension in the room was noticeable, the fear became a living, breathing thing that threatened to suffocate them all.

Daniel and Sarah were stationed by the entrance to the inn, their expressions grim as they kept watch. Emma sat near Margaret, her eyes wide and filled with anxiety, her hands twisting nervously in her lap. The reality of their situation had settled over them all like a heavy fog, and the uncertainty of what might come next only added to the oppressive atmosphere.

"We need to stay sharp," Charles said, his voice breaking the silence. "We can't afford to relax even a little."

Clara nodded, her fingers tapping restlessly on the arm of her chair. "Do you think whoever did this is still out there? Watching us?"

Charles's eyes narrowed slightly as he considered the question. "It's possible. If they wanted to trap us here, they'd need to keep an eye on us to make sure we didn't try anything."

"But why would they flatten our tires and leave us here?" Emma asked, her voice trembling. "Why not just... do whatever they're planning to do and get it over with?"

Margaret opened her eyes, her expression haunted. "Because they want to scare us. They want to make us feel helpless."

"They want control," Clara added, her voice steady despite the fear nagging at her. "Whoever did this, they want to break us down, make us desperate. It's easier to control people when they're scared and panicking."

Daniel shifted in his seat, his jaw clenched. "Well, I'm not giving them the satisfaction. They're not going to break us."

Sarah nodded in agreement, though her eyes betrayed her unease. "We just need to keep our wits about us. If we stay calm and think things through, we'll figure a way out of this."

Clara appreciated their determination, but she couldn't shake the feeling that time was running out. The night seemed endless, and with each passing hour, the sense of dread grew stronger. They were trapped in the inn, cut off from the outside world, with no way to call for help and no way to escape. The realization that they were at the mercy of an unseen threat was almost too much to bear.

Suddenly, the faint sound of movement outside the blocked door caught Clara's attention. It was a soft, almost imperceptible sound—like the crunch of snow underfoot, or the rustle of fabric against wood. Her heart leapt into her throat, and she instinctively reached for the small knife she had taken from the kitchen earlier. It wasn't much, but it was better than nothing.

"Did you hear that?" she whispered, her eyes locking onto Charles's.

He nodded, his expression darkening as he rose from his chair. "Stay here. I'll check it out."

"No," Clara said quickly, standing up as well. "I'm coming with you."

Charles hesitated, his eyes searching hers for a moment before he nodded. "Okay. But stay close."

They moved toward the door as quietly as they could, the tension thickening with every step. Clara's heart pounded in her chest, her pulse racing as they reached the door. Charles pressed his ear against the wood, his expression tense as he listened.

The silence stretched on, the only sound the crackling of the fire behind them. Clara held her breath, waiting for something—anything—that would explain what she had heard. But there was nothing. Just the oppressive stillness of the night.

Charles pulled back from the door, his brow furrowed. "I don't hear anything now. Maybe it was just the wind."

Clara wanted to believe him, but the unease in her gut refused to let go. "Maybe. But I'm not sure we can trust anything right now."

Charles nodded in agreement. "You're right. We need to stay vigilant."

They returned to the group, and Clara noticed how everyone seemed to be on edge, their nerves frayed by the constant tension. Even the smallest sound or movement was enough to send a jolt of fear through them, and Clara knew that if this continued, their resolve might start to crumble.

Margaret shifted uncomfortably on the sofa, her voice barely above a whisper. "How long can we keep this up? We're exhausted, and whoever's out there… they're just waiting for us to make a mistake."

Charles sighed, running a hand through his hair. "We'll keep rotating watches. We can't afford to sleep all at once, but we'll take turns resting. We have to conserve our energy."

Clara nodded, though she knew that resting would be difficult under the circumstances. Every time she closed her eyes, she could see Alex's lifeless body lying in the snow, the list of names with their fates already decided. The weight of the unknown pressed down on her, making it hard to breathe.

Hours passed in a blur of tense silence, the night dragging on with agonizing slowness. Clara took her turn on watch, her eyes scanning the darkened room for any signs of movement, her ears straining to catch the faintest sound. The minutes ticked by, each one feeling like an eternity, until finally, she felt her eyelids growing heavy.

Just as she was about to drift off, a loud crash echoed through the inn, jolting her awake. She jumped to her feet, her heart racing as she looked around in confusion.

"What was that?" Emma gasped, her voice trembling with fear.

Clara's pulse quickened as she glanced at Charles, who was

already moving toward the source of the noise. "Stay here," he said firmly. "I'll check it out."

"No," Clara said again, her voice stronger this time. "We all go together. We're safer in numbers."

Charles hesitated, but then nodded. "Alright. Let's move."

They moved cautiously through the inn, their footsteps barely making a sound on the old wooden floors. The crash had come from the direction of the dining room, and as they approached, Clara's heart pounded in her chest.

When they reached the dining room, Clara's breath caught in her throat. The room was in shambles. Chairs had been overturned, dishes smashed on the floor, and the curtains torn from their rods. The large window at the far end of the room had been shattered, the cold night air seeping in through the jagged opening.

"Someone was in here," Daniel said, his voice filled with dread. "They were inside."

"But why didn't we hear them earlier?" Emma asked, her voice shaking. "Why wait until now?"

"Maybe they were testing us," Clara suggested, her mind racing. "Seeing how we'd react."

Charles moved toward the broken window, his expression grim. "Or maybe they were trying to send a message."

The sight of the shattered glass sent a wave of fear through Clara, but she forced herself to stay calm. Whoever had done this was trying to rattle them, to make them panic. But they couldn't afford to let fear control them.

"We need to fix this," Clara said, her voice steady despite the fear gnawing at her. "We can't leave the window open like this. It's too dangerous."

Margaret nodded, her hands trembling as she began gathering the fallen curtains. "We can use these to cover the opening, at least for now."

The group worked quickly to block the broken window, using the curtains and whatever else they could find to seal the gap. The cold air still seeped in, but it was better than leaving the room exposed.

As they finished securing the window, Clara noticed something on the floor near the shattered glass. It was a small, folded piece of paper, partially hidden beneath a chair. Her heart skipped a beat as she reached down to pick it up, her hands trembling slightly.

"What is it?" Sarah asked, her voice tense.

Clara unfolded the paper, her breath catching in her throat as she read the words written in neat, precise handwriting:

You can't hide forever.

Clara's blood ran cold as she stared at the message. The words were simple, but the threat behind them was unmistakable. Whoever had broken into the inn knew they were inside, and they were toying with them, waiting for the right moment to strike.

"They know we're here," Clara said, her voice trembling with a mix of fear and anger. "They're watching us."

Charles took the note from her, his expression darkening as he read the message. "This changes everything. They're not just trying to scare us—they're planning something."

"But what?" Daniel asked, his voice filled with dread. "What do they want?"

Clara's mind raced as she tried to make sense of it all. The list of names, Alex's death, the flattened tires, and now this. The pieces of the puzzle were starting to come together, but the picture they formed was terrifying.

"They want control," Clara said, her voice steady despite the terror spreading inside of her. "They want to break us down, make us feel helpless, so that when they do make their move, we won't be able to fight back."

Margaret's face had gone pale, her hands shaking as she clutched the edges of the makeshift curtain they had used to block the window. "But what do we do? How can we fight back if we don't even know who they are?"

Charles's jaw tightened as he looked around the room, his eyes filled with determination. "We fight back by staying strong, by not letting them see our fear. We stick together, and we watch each other's backs. Whatever they're planning, we won't let them win."

The group nodded in agreement, though Clara could see the fear still lingering in their eyes. The situation was spiraling out of control, and they were running out of options. But she knew they couldn't afford to give up. They had to keep fighting, no matter how hopeless it seemed.

As they returned to the lounge, Clara couldn't shake the feeling that someone—or something—was lurking in the shadows, waiting for the right moment to strike. The inn, once a place of warmth and safety, now felt like a prison, the walls closing in around them with each passing moment.

They took turns on watch, each person doing their best to stay alert despite the exhaustion that was beginning to take its toll. The hours dragged on, the night seeming to stretch endlessly, until finally, the faint light of dawn began to creep through the blocked windows.

Clara sat by the fire, her eyes heavy with fatigue, but her mind still racing. The fear was a constant, gnawing presence, but beneath it was a growing determination. They had to survive this. They had to find a way out.

As the first rays of sunlight filtered through the cracks in the curtains, Clara felt a glimmer of hope. The night had been long and terrifying, but they had made it through. They were still alive, still together, and that was something.

But she knew the danger was far from over. The message on the note had been clear: their enemies were still out there, watching, waiting. The threat was real, and they couldn't afford to let their guard down.

"We made it through the night," Charles said quietly, his voice breaking the silence. "But we're not out of the woods yet."

Clara nodded, her resolve hardening. "We need to keep moving forward. We need to find a way to turn the tables on them."

"And we will," Charles said firmly. "We'll figure this out, Clara. We'll find a way to fight back."

Clara looked into his eyes, seeing the determination there, and felt a spark of hope. They were in this together, and as long as they stood united, they had a chance.

The dawn had come, but the storm within the inn was far from over. The unseen threat still loomed over them, and the fear of what might come next gnawed at Clara's every thought. But she refused to let it consume her.

They would survive this. They had to. And whatever secrets the inn held, whatever dangers awaited them, they would face it head-on, together.

11

Chapter 11

The faint light of dawn crept through the curtains, casting a muted glow over the room. The fire in the hearth had burned down to embers, leaving the lounge in an eerie half-light that only added to the sense of unease that hung over them all. Clara sat in the same chair she had occupied through the long, sleepless night, her mind racing as she tried to piece together the events of the past hours.

They had survived the night, but the threat was far from over. The note they had found in the dining room, the shattered window, and the relentless fear that had gripped them all told Clara that they were still in grave danger. Whoever was out there, watching them, wasn't done with them yet. And the worst part was, they had no idea who it was or what they wanted.

Charles moved quietly around the room, his eyes sharp and alert as he checked the barricades they had set up the night before. His face was drawn, the lines of exhaustion etched deeply into his features, but his determination had not wavered. Clara knew he was just as scared as the rest of them, but he was doing his best to stay strong, to keep everyone focused.

Margaret was sitting near the fire, her hands wrapped around a cup of lukewarm tea. She looked pale and tired, but there was a steely resolve in her eyes that Clara hadn't seen before. The events of the night had shaken her, but they had also brought out a strength that Clara hadn't expected.

Emma, Sarah, and Daniel were gathered near the windows, their faces tense as they watched the snow-covered landscape outside. The night had been a test of their endurance, and while they had all made it through, the fear of what might come next was palpable.

Clara was about to suggest that they take a moment to regroup, to come up with a plan for the day, when Daniel suddenly froze, his eyes narrowing as he stared at something near the ceiling.

"What is it?" Clara asked, her voice tinged with concern.

Daniel didn't answer right away. Instead, he moved closer to the wall, his gaze fixed on a small, almost imperceptible object tucked into the corner where the ceiling met the wall. He reached up, carefully pulling the object free, and turned back to the group, his expression a mix of confusion and anger.

"It's a camera," he said, his voice low and filled with disbelief.

Clara's heart skipped a beat as she stared at the small black device in Daniel's hand. It was a tiny camera, barely noticeable unless you were looking for it, with a small lens that had been trained on the lounge.

"They've been watching us," Sarah whispered, her voice trembling with fear. "This whole time, they've been watching us."

Charles moved quickly to Daniel's side, his eyes narrowing as he examined the camera. "How long has this been here?" he asked, his voice filled with tension.

Daniel shook his head, his expression dark. "I don't know. But if this is here, there might be more."

Clara felt a cold shiver run down her spine. The idea that someone had been watching them, monitoring their every move, was almost too terrifying to comprehend. But she couldn't afford to let the fear paralyze her. They had to find out how many cameras there were and figure out who had put them there.

"We need to search the entire inn," Clara said, her voice steady despite the fear gnawing at her. "There could be more cameras, more places where they're watching us. We have to find them all."

Charles nodded in agreement, his expression serious. "We'll split up again, but this time we'll stay in pairs. Check every room, every corner. If there are more cameras, we need to find them."

The group quickly divided into pairs: Clara with Charles, Sarah with Emma, and Daniel with Margaret. They moved through the inn with a renewed sense of urgency, the fear of being watched driving them to be thorough, to leave no stone unturned.

Clara and Charles started in the lounge, carefully checking every corner, every crevice where a camera could be hidden. Clara's heart raced as she moved from one spot to the next, her mind reeling with the implications of what they had found. If there were cameras in the lounge, there could be cameras in their rooms, in the bathrooms… everywhere.

"What kind of person does this?" Clara asked quietly, her

voice filled with a mixture of fear and anger. "Who watches people like this?"

"Someone who wants control," Charles replied, his tone grim. "Someone who wants to know our every move, to see how we react, how we're holding up."

Clara felt a surge of anger at the thought. The idea that someone had been watching them, manipulating them, made her blood boil. But beneath the anger was a deep-seated fear, the knowledge that they were dealing with someone who was far more dangerous and calculating than they had realized.

They found another camera hidden behind a painting in the lounge, its lens trained on the seating area where they had spent most of the night. Charles carefully removed it, his expression darkening as he examined the device.

"These are professional-grade cameras," he said, his voice laced with suspicion. "Whoever set these up knew what they were doing."

Clara's mind raced as she tried to make sense of it all. "But why? What are they trying to accomplish by watching us?"

Charles shook his head, his brow furrowed in concentration. "Maybe they're looking for something. Or maybe they're just trying to keep us off balance, to make us feel like we're under constant surveillance."

Clara shuddered at the thought. The idea that someone was watching their every move, analyzing their behavior, sent a wave of fear crashing over her. But she couldn't let the fear consume her. They had to stay focused, had to find the rest of the cameras and figure out who was behind this.

As they continued their search, Clara's mind kept returning to Alex. Had he known about the cameras? Had he been involved in setting them up, or had he been as much a victim as they were? The questions gnawed at her, but there were no easy answers.

After thoroughly searching the lounge, Clara and Charles moved on to the dining room, where they had found the note earlier. The room was still in disarray, the broken window covered by the makeshift barricade they had set up during the night. Clara felt a surge of anxiety as they stepped inside, the memory of the note's chilling message still fresh in her mind.

They quickly found another camera hidden in the corner near the ceiling, its lens pointed toward the center of the room. Charles carefully removed it, his expression grim as he added it to the growing collection of devices they had found.

"How many more of these do you think there are?" Clara asked, her voice tinged with dread.

"I don't know," Charles admitted, his tone filled with frustration. "But we have to find them all. We can't leave any of them active."

They moved through the inn with methodical precision, checking every room, every hallway, every corner where a camera could be hidden. The fear of being watched drove them to be thorough, to leave no stone unturned. Each new camera they found only added to the sense of dread that hung over them, the knowledge that they were being monitored at all times, even in their most private moments.

In the kitchen, they found a camera hidden inside one of the cupboards, its lens positioned to watch the entire room. In the bedrooms, they discovered tiny cameras embedded in the walls, their lenses barely visible unless you were specifically looking for them. Even the bathrooms weren't spared—small, almost invisible cameras were hidden in the corners, their lenses trained on the shower and sink.

Clara felt a sickening sense of violation as they removed each camera, the realization that their privacy had been completely stripped away almost too much to bear. The inn, once a place of safety and refuge, had become a dungeon, its walls hiding a multitude of secrets.

When they regrouped in the lounge, the pile of cameras on the coffee table was a stark reminder of just how much control their unseen enemy had over them. The fear and anger that had been simmering beneath the surface now threatened to boil over, but Clara knew they couldn't afford to lose their composure. They had to stay focused, had to figure out what to do next.

"This is insane," Sarah said, her voice trembling with anger. "Whoever did this… they've been watching us the whole time. Every conversation, every move we've made… they've seen it all."

Margaret looked pale, her hands trembling as she stared at the cameras. "But why? Why go to all this trouble? What do they want from us?"

"They want control," Charles repeated, his voice steady but filled with underlying tension. "They want to make us feel like we're powerless, like we're being hunted."

"But we're not powerless," Clara said firmly, her resolve hardening. "We found the cameras. We know they're watching us, and we can use that to our advantage."

Daniel frowned, his expression skeptical. "How? They're the ones in control. They know our every move before we even make it."

"Not if we outsmart them," Clara said, her mind racing with possibilities. "We know where the cameras were, and we know they've been watching us. But if we act like we don't know, we might be able to trick them, make them think we're still in the dark."

Charles nodded, a glimmer of hope in his eyes. "We can set a trap. Make them think we're doing one thing while we're actually doing something else."

"But we have to be careful," Emma added, her voice trembling with fear. "If they realize we're onto them… they might make their move."

Clara's mind raced as she considered the options. The idea of turning the tables on their unseen enemy was both terrifying and exhilarating, but she knew the risks were high. One wrong move, one misstep, and they could all be in even greater danger.

"We need to figure out who's behind this," Clara said, her voice filled with determination. "The cameras, the flattened tires, the note… it all has to be connected. If we can figure out who's pulling the strings, we might be able to stop them."

Charles nodded in agreement. "We should start by examining the cameras themselves. There might be something in the footage that gives us a clue."

"Or the cameras themselves might have something," Daniel suggested. "A brand, a manufacturer, something we can trace."

Clara felt a surge of determination. They were no longer passive victims in this twisted game; they were taking control, fighting back. The fear that had gripped her since the discovery of the cameras was still there, but now it was tempered by a growing resolve.

The group quickly got to work, examining the cameras they had collected. Charles and Daniel carefully dismantled a few of the devices, searching for any identifying marks or clues that might point to their origin. Sarah and Emma sifted through the pile, checking for anything that might have been overlooked.

As they worked, Clara couldn't shake the feeling that they were on borrowed time. The discovery of the cameras had shifted the balance of power, but she knew their enemies wouldn't sit idly by. They would strike back, and when they did, they had to be ready.

Hours passed as they meticulously searched for clues, the tension in the room thickening with every passing minute. The sun had fully risen, casting a pale light through the curtains, but the sense of foreboding that had settled over the inn refused to lift.

Finally, Charles straightened up, holding a small circuit board in his hand. "I found something," he said, his voice filled with urgency.

The group quickly gathered around him, their eyes fixed on the tiny piece of technology in his hand. "What is it?" Clara asked, her heart pounding in her chest.

"It's a transmitter," Charles explained, his expression serious. "These cameras weren't just recording us—they were transmitting the footage somewhere else."

Clara's blood ran cold at the revelation. "You mean… someone was watching us in real-time?"

Charles nodded, his face grim. "That's what it looks like. Whoever set these up has been watching us live, monitoring everything we do."

"But where were they transmitting to?" Sarah asked, her voice filled with dread. "Can we trace it?"

Charles hesitated. "It's possible, but it won't be easy. We'd need to find the receiver, the device that was picking up the signal. Without that, we're shooting in the dark."

Clara felt a wave of frustration wash over her. They were so close to finding out who was behind this, but the pieces of the puzzle were still just out of reach. "Then we need to find the receiver. It has to be close by, right? Within range of the inn?"

"Most likely," Charles agreed. "But it could be hidden anywhere. Inside the inn, outside… we don't know."

"We'll have to search the inn again," Clara said, her voice filled with determination. "Top to bottom, every inch. If the receiver is here, we'll find it."

The group nodded in agreement, their resolve hardening. They were in a race against time, and every second counted. The knowledge that their enemy had been watching them in real-time, monitoring their every move, only fueled their determination to fight back.

As they prepared to search the inn once more, Clara couldn't shake the feeling that they were being watched even now, that their enemies were one step ahead of them. But she refused to let the fear consume her. They had made it through the night, and they would make it through whatever came next.

The search was slow and meticulous, every room, every hallway, every corner of the inn scoured for any sign of the receiver. The fear of being watched drove them to be thorough. But as the hours passed, their search turned up nothing.

Clara's frustration grew with each empty room, each fruitless search. The receiver had to be somewhere, but the inn was large, with countless nooks and crannies where it could be hidden. And the longer they searched, the more the fear gnawed at her, the knowledge that their enemies were still out there, watching, waiting.

Finally, as the sun began to dip below the horizon, casting long shadows across the snow-covered landscape, they gathered in the lounge once more, their expressions grim.

"We didn't find anything," Daniel said, his voice filled with frustration. "It's like they've disappeared."

Clara shook her head, refusing to give up. "They're still out there. They're watching us, waiting for us to make a mistake."

"But what if the receiver isn't in the inn?" Margaret asked, her voice trembling. "What if it's outside, somewhere we can't find it?"

Charles frowned, his expression thoughtful. "It's possible. But if it's outside, it would have to be close by. The signal wouldn't travel far in this weather."

Clara's mind raced as she considered the possibilities. "Then we need to widen our search. If it's outside, it could be hidden in the woods, or even in one of the outbuildings."

"Or it could be buried in the snow," Emma added, her voice filled with dread. "We might never find it."

Clara felt a surge of frustration, but she knew Emma was right. The receiver could be anywhere, and the thought of searching the entire area, especially with the snow still thick on the ground, was daunting. But they couldn't give up. They had to keep searching, keep fighting.

"We'll start searching outside at first light," Charles said, his tone filled with determination. "We'll check the woods, the outbuildings, anywhere it could be hidden."

Clara nodded, though the thought of venturing outside, into the cold and the snow, filled her with a sense of dread. But they had no choice. If they wanted to find the receiver, they had to keep searching.

As they settled in for another long night, the fear of being watched still gnawed at Clara. The discovery of the cameras had changed everything, but the threat was far from over. Their enemies were still out there, watching, waiting, and Clara knew they had to be ready for whatever came next.

They would survive this. They had to. And they would find the answers they needed, no matter what it took.

But as the shadows lengthened and the night closed in around them once more, Clara couldn't shake the feeling that time was running out. The storm had passed, but the danger was far from over.

12

Chapter 12

The night had been long, filled with tension that pressed down on everyone in the inn like a weight too heavy to bear. Clara barely slept, her thoughts racing with possibilities and plans as the dread washed over her. The discovery of the hidden cameras had shifted everything. Knowing they were being watched, that their every move had been monitored, left her feeling vulnerable and exposed. But it also fueled her determination to fight back, to regain control of a situation that had spiraled far beyond what any of them could have imagined.

As the first light of dawn filtered through the heavy curtains, casting a faint glow over the room, Clara finally stirred from the chair where she had spent most of the night. Her muscles were stiff, her body aching from the tension and lack of sleep, but she pushed the discomfort aside. They had work to do.

The others were already awake, their faces drawn and pale, the exhaustion of the past few days clearly taking its toll. Charles was at the table, studying the dismantled cameras with a focused intensity, while Daniel and Margaret prepared what little food they had left for breakfast. Sarah and Emma were by the window, peering out into the cold, snow-covered landscape, their expressions tense and wary.

"Morning," Clara said quietly, her voice rough from disuse.

Charles looked up from his work, his eyes weary but resolute. "Morning. We need to get moving soon. The sooner we find that receiver, the better."

Clara nodded, her resolve hardening. "Agreed. We'll start outside as soon as we're ready."

They ate a quick breakfast, the food tasteless in the face of fear. Conversation was sparse, each of them lost in their own thoughts, but the sense of unity was still there, a shared determination to see this through to the end.

After they finished eating, the group bundled up in their warmest clothes, preparing to venture out into the cold. The snow had stopped falling during the night, leaving behind a pristine, white landscape that seemed almost peaceful in its stillness. But Clara knew better. The tranquility was an illusion, masking the danger that lurked just beneath the surface.

As they stepped outside, the cold air bit at their skin, the snow crunching underfoot as they moved cautiously through the inn's yard. The plan was simple: they would search the area around the inn, starting with the most obvious places where the receiver could be hidden. The outbuildings, the woods, and any other location that provided cover.

The air was thick with tension, each of them acutely aware of the stakes. They were on the clock, and they knew their enemies were likely watching their every move. But the fear only fueled Clara's determination. They had to find the receiver, had to stop whoever was behind this before it was too late.

They started with the outbuildings—a small shed and a garage that housed an old snowmobile and various tools. The shed was locked, but Charles quickly pried the door open with a crowbar they had brought from the inn. Inside, the shed was dark and cramped, filled with old gardening tools, bags of salt, and other odds and ends that had accumulated over the years. The inside was dimly lit by the morning light filtering through the windows, revealing an old snowmobile covered in a thick layer of dust, along with several shelves filled with tools, oil cans, and other equipment.

Clara's heart pounded as they searched the shed, her hands trembling slightly as she moved items aside, checking for any sign of the receiver. The fear of what they might find ate away at her, but she pushed it down, focusing on the task at hand.

"There's nothing here," Daniel said after a few minutes, his voice laced with frustration. "Just junk."

"Let's check the garage," Charles suggested, his tone steady despite the tension in the air.

They moved to the garage, the large, wooden door creaking loudly as Charles pulled it open. Clara's eyes scanned the room, searching for anything out of place. The receiver had to be somewhere nearby; they just had to find it. The anxiety clawed at her, but she forced herself to stay calm, to focus.

They searched the garage methodically, checking every shelf, every corner, but there was no sign of the receiver. The frustration was beginning to mount, the fear that they were running out of time nagging at Clara's resolve.

"Maybe it's not in one of the outbuildings," Emma suggested, her voice trembling slightly. "Maybe it's hidden in the woods, or buried in the snow."

"Or it could be near the cars," Sarah added, her brow furrowed in thought. "If they wanted to monitor us as we came and went, that would be the perfect spot."

Clara's heart skipped a beat at the suggestion. It made sense. The cars were the one place they hadn't thoroughly checked, and if the receiver was there, it would explain why they hadn't found it yet.

"Let's check the cars," Clara said, her voice filled with urgency. "We can't afford to overlook anything."

The group moved quickly toward the area where their vehicles were parked, the snow crunching loudly underfoot as they approached. The cars were still there, their tires slashed and deflated, the sight a grim reminder of how isolated they were. The cold seemed to seep into Clara's bones as they approached her car, the anxiety swelling up in her, but she refused to let it paralyze her.

Charles started with the first car, checking under the wheel wells and beneath the chassis, while Daniel did the same with another vehicle. Clara moved to her own car, her breath catching in her throat as she crouched down to inspect the undercarriage.

At first, there was nothing—just snow and the dark, dirty underside of the car. But then she noticed something out of place, a small black box attached to the frame just behind the front bumper. Her heart skipped a beat as she reached out, her gloved fingers brushing against the cold metal surface.

"I think I found something," Clara called out, her voice trembling with a mix of fear and excitement.

The others quickly gathered around her, their breath visible in the cold air as they crouched down to see what she had found. Charles reached out, carefully prying the box free from its position beneath the car. It was small and black, with a faint red light blinking on one side.

"This is it," Charles said, his voice filled with a mixture of relief and tension. "This is the receiver."

Clara's heart pounded in her chest as she stared at the device. The blinking light seemed to mock them, a silent reminder of the danger they were in. But finding the receiver was a victory, however small. It meant they were no longer completely in the dark. They had a piece of the puzzle, and now they had to figure out what to do with it.

"What now?" Sarah asked, her voice tinged with anxiety. "What do we do with it?"

Charles examined the receiver closely. "We need to disable it. If this is what's been transmitting the footage from the cameras, we have to cut off the signal."

"But won't they know we've found it?" Emma asked, her voice trembling. "Won't they realize we've disabled it?"

Clara felt a cold knot of fear in her stomach, but she knew they couldn't afford to hesitate. Disabling the receiver was a risk, but leaving it active was even more dangerous. They had to take control, had to stop their enemies from watching them.

"We don't have a choice," Clara said firmly. "We can't let them keep watching us. We have to disable it."

Charles nodded in agreement, his expression grim. "I'll disconnect the power source. That should cut the signal."

He carefully pried open the casing of the receiver, exposing a small battery and circuit board inside. With practiced precision, Charles disconnected the battery, the faint red light on the receiver flickering and then going dark.

A tense silence followed, the weight of their actions hanging heavy in the cold morning air. Clara felt a surge of relief at seeing the light go out, but the fear was still there, a constant, growing presence that refused to let go.

"Do you think that did it?" Margaret asked, her voice barely above a whisper.

"It should have," Charles replied, his tone filled with cautious optimism. "Without power, the receiver can't transmit the signal. Whoever's been watching us won't be able to see what we're doing anymore."

"But what if they come looking for it?" Daniel asked, his voice tinged with concern. "What if they realize we've disabled it and come after us?"

Clara's mind raced with the possibilities. The thought of their enemies discovering what they had done, of them retaliating, was terrifying. But she knew they couldn't afford to dwell on it. They had taken a step in the right direction, and now they had to be ready for whatever came next.

"We'll be ready for them," Clara said, her voice filled with determination. "If they come looking for the receiver, we'll be waiting."

Charles nodded in agreement, his expression serious. "We need to get back to the inn. We can plan our next move from there."

The group quickly made their way back to the inn, the cold biting at their skin as they moved through the snow. The tension in the air was thick, each of them acutely aware that their enemies could be watching, could be closing in at any moment. But the fear only fueled Clara's resolve. They had taken a step toward regaining control, and she was determined to see it through to the end.

Once inside the inn, they gathered in the lounge, the fire in the hearth doing little to chase away the chill that had settled over them all. The receiver sat on the table between them, a small but significant victory in their battle against the unseen threat that loomed over them.

"We need to be smart about this," Charles said, his tone serious. "Disabling the receiver was the right move, but we have to be prepared for the possibility that our enemies will retaliate."

"They might already be on their way," Daniel said, his voice tense. "We need to be ready for anything."

Clara nodded, her mind racing with possibilities. "We need to secure the inn even more than we already have. Block every entrance, cover every window. If they come for us, we have to make it as difficult as possible for them to get inside."

Margaret's face was pale, but there was a steely resolve in her eyes. "We should also set up a lookout. If anyone approaches the inn, we need to know about it right away."

"I'll take the first watch," Emma volunteered, her voice filled with determination. "I'm not going to let them take us by surprise."

Clara felt a surge of pride at Emma's bravery. They were all scared, but they were facing that fear head-on, refusing to be broken by it. It was a small comfort in the face of everything they were up against, but it was enough to keep Clara focused.

As they worked together to secure the inn, blocking doors and windows, setting up lookouts, Clara couldn't shake the feeling that they were still being watched, that their enemies were already closing in. The horror tearing away at her, but she refused to let it consume her. They had made it through the night, and they had taken a step toward regaining control. But the battle was far from over.

Hours passed in a blur of tense activity, the fear of what

might come next driving them to be thorough, to leave nothing to chance. They fortified the inn as best they could, using whatever materials were available to block the entrances and cover the windows. Every creak of the floorboards, every rustle of the wind outside sent a jolt of fear through Clara, but she pushed it down, focusing on the task at hand.

By the time they finished, the sun was already dipping below the horizon, casting long shadows across the snow-covered landscape. The inn was as secure as they could make it, but the fear of what might come next hung heavy in the air.

They gathered in the lounge once more, the fire crackling softly in the hearth. Clara could see the exhaustion in everyone's faces, the toll of the past days weighing heavily on them all. But there was also a sense of determination, a resolve to see this through no matter what it took.

"We've done everything we can," Charles said, his voice filled with a mixture of exhaustion and resolve. "Now we wait. If they come for us, we'll be ready."

Clara nodded. The knowledge that their enemies were out there, watching, waiting, was almost too much to bear. But she knew they couldn't afford to give in to fear. They had to stay strong, had to stay focused.

As the night settled in around them, Clara took her turn on watch, her eyes scanning the darkened room for any signs of movement, her ears straining to catch the faintest sound. The minutes ticked by, each one feeling like an eternity, until finally, she felt her eyelids growing heavy.

But just as she was about to drift off, a faint sound outside the inn caught her attention—a soft crunch, like footsteps in the snow. Her heart leapt into her throat, and she instinctively reached for the small knife. It wasn't much, but it was better than nothing.

She strained to listen, her pulse quickening as the sound grew louder, closer. Someone was out there, moving through the snow toward the inn. The fear clawed at her, but she forced herself to stay calm, to focus.

She quickly alerted the others, their faces tense and pale as they listened to the approaching footsteps. The sound was faint, almost imperceptible, but it was there—a steady, deliberate rhythm that sent a shiver down Clara's spine.

"They're here," she whispered, her voice trembling with a mix of fear and resolve. "They're coming for us."

Charles's expression darkened, his jaw tightening as he reached for the crowbar he had used earlier. "Get ready," he said, his voice low and filled with determination. "We're not going down without a fight."

Clara's heart pounded in her chest as they moved into position, their makeshift weapons clutched tightly in their hands. The fear was a constant presence, but beneath it was a growing determination. They had come this far, and they weren't going to give up now.

The footsteps grew louder, closer, until they seemed to be right outside the inn. Clara held her breath, her pulse racing as she waited for the inevitable sound of the door being forced open, for the attackers to burst inside.

But then the footsteps stopped.

The silence that followed was deafening, the tension in the air so thick it was almost suffocating. Clara strained to listen, her heart pounding in her ears, but there was nothing—just the heavy, oppressive silence.

"What's happening?" Margaret whispered, her voice trembling with fear.

"I don't know," Clara replied, her voice barely audible. "But we can't let our guard down."

They waited in tense silence, every nerve on edge, but the footsteps did not return. The oppressive stillness of the night settled over them once more, but the fear of what might come next refused to let go.

"They're testing us," Charles said quietly, his voice filled with suspicion. "They're trying to rattle us, to make us jumpy."

"They're doing a good job," Daniel muttered, his grip on the crowbar tightening.

Clara nodded, though her bravery was slowly diminishing. The attackers were out there, waiting, watching, but they weren't making their move—at least, not yet. They were playing a game, a deadly game of cat and mouse, and Clara knew they had to be ready for anything.

"We can't let them get to us," Clara said firmly, her voice steady despite the fear in her chest. "We have to stay focused, stay strong."

Charles nodded in agreement, his expression grim. "We'll take turns on watch, just like before. If they try to get inside, we'll be ready."

The group exchanged tense glances, but no one argued. They knew what they were up against, and they knew the stakes. The night stretched on, the tension thickening with every passing minute, but they refused to let fear control them.

As Clara took her turn on watch, her eyes scanning the darkened room, she couldn't shake the feeling that their enemies were still out there, waiting for the right moment to strike. The distress tormented her, but she refused to let it consume her.

They had made it through the night before, and they would

make it through this one too. They had to. The fight for control was far from over, but Clara was determined to see it through to the end—no matter what it took.

13

Chapter 13

The night was suffocating in its silence, the kind that pressed down on the chest and made it hard to breathe. Clara kept her eyes fixed on the windows, the barricades they'd set up in front of the doors, and the dark corners of the room that seemed to stretch on endlessly. Every shadow looked like a threat, every sound a potential danger. The tension was electric, sparking across their small group like a live wire.

Charles stood by the door, his body rigid, every muscle coiled tight. He had taken to gripping the crowbar like a lifeline, his knuckles white as he stared out into the darkness. His focus was unyielding, but the lines around his eyes betrayed the exhaustion creeping in. They were all tired. They hadn't slept more than a few minutes at a time, constantly trading off watch duties, knowing that any lapse could mean the end.

Emma was the one who seemed the most affected by the pressure. She paced near the fire, her movements restless and erratic, her fingers twisting the hem of her sweater as if she could unravel the anxiety from her mind. Clara watched her for a moment, feeling a pang of concern. Emma had been strong—stronger than Clara would have expected—but there was something in her eyes now, a distant look that suggested the burden of the situation was becoming too much.

Sarah and Margaret sat near the fireplace, whispering quietly to one another, their voices barely audible over the crackling flames. Daniel leaned against the wall, eyes closed but body tense, like a spring ready to snap. They were all on edge, waiting for something to happen. And Clara knew it was only a matter of time.

The hours dragged by with an agonizing slowness. Outside, the snow continued to fall, a steady blanket that seemed to mute the world around them. Inside, the air was thick, charged with anticipation. Every creak of the old wooden floorboards, every groan of the wind against the walls sent shivers down their spines. They were trapped in a waiting game, and the pressure was becoming unbearable.

Then it happened.

A loud crash shattered the tense quiet, followed by the unmistakable sound of wood splintering. Clara's heart lurched as the door to the kitchen flew open with a force that sent it crashing against the wall. The room erupted into chaos. Charles was the first to react, surging forward with the crowbar raised high, but the intruder was quick—too quick.

The man who had broken in was dressed in dark clothing, his face obscured by a balaclava. He moved with precision, shoving Charles aside and heading straight for the others. There was no hesitation, no uncertainty in his actions. This was a man who knew what he was doing.

"Get back!" Charles shouted, recovering quickly and lunging

at the intruder.

Clara grabbed the closest thing she could find—a heavy candlestick from the mantle—and rushed to help. The attacker swung around, catching her movement out of the corner of his eye. He lashed out, the force of the blow sending Clara stumbling backward, pain exploding in her side.

"Clara!" Emma screamed, her voice shrill with panic.

Daniel and Sarah were on their feet now, trying to corner the intruder, but he was fast and ruthless. He dodged and weaved, grabbing hold of Margaret and using her as a shield. The move was so swift and brutal that it took everyone by surprise.

"Let her go!" Charles roared, advancing with renewed fury.

Margaret gasped, her eyes wide with terror as the man tightened his grip on her. Clara could see the cold calculation in the intruder's eyes, the way he assessed each of them, planning his next move. They were outmatched, and he knew it.

But something changed. Perhaps it was the sight of Margaret's fear, the realization that they had no other choice, or maybe it was just pure survival instinct. Whatever it was, Charles didn't hesitate. He swung the crowbar with all his strength, aiming for the man's head.

The sound of metal connecting with bone was sickening, a dull thud that reverberated through the room. The intruder's grip on Margaret loosened, and she wrenched herself free, stumbling toward Clara. The man staggered, his balance faltering as blood began to seep from the wound on his temple.

Charles didn't stop. He struck again and again, each blow fueled by desperation. The intruder went down hard, collapsing to the floor in a lifeless heap. The room fell into a stunned silence, broken only by the ragged breaths of those who had just fought for their lives.

Clara dropped the candlestick, her hands shaking uncontrollably. She stared at the crumpled body on the floor, the blood pooling around it, and felt a wave of nausea rise in her throat. The reality of what they had just done hit her with full force. They had killed a man.

But there was no time to dwell on it. No time to process what had just happened. Margaret was sobbing quietly, clutching at Clara's arm, and Charles was breathing heavily, his face pale and splattered with blood. Daniel and Sarah stood frozen, their eyes wide with shock.

Then Clara noticed something. Or rather, she noticed the absence of something.

"Where's Emma?" she asked, her voice barely above a whisper.

Everyone's heads snapped up, their eyes darting around the room, searching for the young woman who had been with them just moments ago. Panic flared in Clara's chest as she realized Emma was nowhere to be seen.

"Emma!" Margaret cried, her voice breaking with fear.

They scrambled to their feet, searching the room, calling her name. But there was no answer. The only sound was the crackling of the fire and the distant howl of the wind outside. Emma was gone.

"She must have run when the man broke in," Sarah said, her voice trembling with uncertainty. "Maybe she got scared and hid somewhere."

"No," Daniel said, shaking his head, his expression dark. "She wouldn't just leave like that. Something's wrong."

Clara's heart raced as the implications of Emma's disappearance sank in. The attacker had been a diversion—a way to draw their attention while someone else took Emma. But who? And why?

"We have to find her," Clara said urgently, her voice steady despite the turmoil inside her. "She can't have gone far."

Charles nodded, still catching his breath, but already focused on the task ahead. "Check the rest of the inn. She might be hiding somewhere. If she's outside..." He didn't finish the sentence, but they all knew what he meant. If Emma was outside in the snow, in the dark, with those people out there... they had to find her fast.

The group quickly split up, searching the inn with a frantic intensity. Clara checked the bedrooms, the bathrooms, every nook and cranny where Emma could have hidden. But there was no sign of her. The fear of what might have happened to Emma weighed heavily on Clara's mind as she moved from room to room, calling her name, hoping against hope that she would answer.

But the inn was silent, the empty rooms offering no clues, no comfort. Clara's worry deepened with each passing minute. Where was Emma? Had she been taken? Was she still alive?

When Clara returned to the lounge, the others were already there, their faces etched with worry and confusion.

"Nothing," Daniel said, frustration evident in his voice. "She's not in the inn."

"She has to be," Margaret insisted, tears streaming down her face. "She wouldn't just leave us like this. She wouldn't..."

Clara put a hand on Margaret's shoulder, trying to offer some comfort, even though her own heart was pounding with anxiety. "We'll find her. We have to."

"Maybe she's outside," Sarah suggested, though her tone was uncertain. "If she was scared, she might have run out into the snow."

Charles looked grim, his jaw set as he weighed their options. "If she's out there, we need to find her now. She won't survive long in this cold, especially not with those people out there."

Clara nodded, already moving toward the door. The thought of Emma out in the freezing cold, alone and terrified, spurred her into action. They had to find her before it was too late.

The group quickly bundled up in their coats and scarves, the cold air biting at their skin as they stepped outside. The night was dark, the snow-covered landscape stretching out before them like a vast, unbroken expanse. The wind howled through the trees, a haunting sound that seemed to echo their own fears.

"Emma!" Clara called out, her voice barely carrying over the wind. "Emma, where are you?"

There was no answer, only the relentless wind and the crunch of snow under their boots. Clara's heart pounded in her chest as they fanned out, searching the area around the inn, their eyes scanning the darkness for any sign of movement.

The snow was deep, slowing their progress as they trudged through the drifts. Clara's breath came in short, sharp gasps, the cold air burning in her lungs. But she didn't stop, didn't slow down. Emma was out there somewhere, and they had to find her.

"Over here!" Daniel's voice cut through the night, filled with urgency.

Clara's heart leapt as she turned toward the sound of his voice. She pushed through the snow, her legs aching from the effort, until she reached Daniel, who was standing near the edge of the woods that bordered the inn's property.

"What is it?" Clara asked, her voice breathless with both

exertion and worry.

Daniel pointed to the ground, where the snow had been disturbed. Clara's eyes widened as she saw the unmistakable signs of a struggle—footprints, deep and erratic, leading away from the inn and into the woods. The tracks were partially covered by fresh snow, but they were still visible, and they told a story that made Clara's blood run cold.

"Someone dragged her," Daniel said, his voice tight with anger. "They took her into the woods."

Clara's stomach twisted at the sight, a wave of nausea threatening to overwhelm her. Emma hadn't just run off in a panic—she had been taken, dragged away by whoever was out there, lurking in the darkness.

"We have to go after her," Clara said, her voice filled with determination. "We can't let them take her."

Charles and the others arrived, their expressions darkening as they took in the scene. There was no hesitation, no debate. They knew what they had to do.

"Let's go," Charles said, his tone grim but resolute. "We don't have much time."

The group plunged into the woods, following the trail of disturbed snow. The trees closed in around them, their branches casting long, twisted shadows in the moonlight. The wind howled through the forest, carrying with it the faint, ominous creaking of branches and the distant call of some unseen creature. The forest felt alive, as if it were watching them, waiting to see what would happen next.

Clara's breath came in ragged gasps as they pushed deeper into the woods, the cold seeping into her bones. But she didn't slow down, didn't stop. The thought of Emma out there, alone and terrified, drove her forward. They had to find her. They had to bring her back.

The tracks led them deeper into the woods, the trees growing thicker, the darkness more oppressive. Clara's heart pounded in her chest, each step heavy with the weight of what they might find. The silence of the forest was broken only by the crunch of snow underfoot and the labored breathing of the group as they pressed on.

Suddenly, the tracks stopped.

Clara halted, her eyes scanning the area in confusion. The tracks led to a small clearing, but there was no sign of Emma, no sign of anyone. It was as if they had vanished into thin air.

"Where did they go?" Sarah asked, her voice trembling with a mix of fear and desperation. "They were right here…"

Clara felt a sinking feeling in her chest as she looked around the clearing. The trees loomed overhead, their branches twisted and gnarled, casting long shadows across the snow. The air was thick, heavy with the sense that something was terribly wrong.

Then she saw it.

In the center of the clearing, partially buried in the snow, was a small, dark object. Clara's heart skipped a beat as she moved closer, her breath catching in her throat as she recognized what it was.

Emma's scarf.

Clara knelt down, her hands trembling as she picked up the scarf, the soft fabric stiff with cold. It was Emma's, the one she had been wearing when they last saw her. The sight of it sent a wave of panic crashing over Clara. Emma was out here, somewhere, and she was in danger.

"They can't be far," Charles said, his voice filled with urgency. "We need to keep moving."

Clara nodded, her resolve hardening. They couldn't give up. They had to find Emma, no matter what it took.

The group pressed on, their pace quickening as they followed the faint traces of the trail. The forest grew darker, the trees closing in around them, but they didn't stop. The fear of what might have happened to Emma, of what might still happen, drove them forward, pushing them to the limits of their endurance.

The tracks grew fainter, harder to follow, but Clara didn't lose hope. She kept her eyes fixed on the ground, searching for any sign, any clue that might lead them to Emma. The cold was relentless, the darkness oppressive, but she refused to let it stop her.

Then, just as they reached the edge of another clearing, they heard it—a faint, muffled cry, carried on the wind.

"Emma!" Clara shouted, her heart leaping with both relief and fear.

The cry came again, closer this time. Clara's pulse quickened as they raced toward the sound, their breath coming in short, sharp gasps as they pushed through the snow. The fear of what they might find, of what might have already happened, was overwhelming, but Clara forced herself to stay focused.

They burst into the clearing, the moonlight casting long shadows across the snow. There, at the far edge of the clearing, was Emma.

She was bound and gagged, her eyes wide with terror as she struggled against the ropes that held her. Clara's heart broke at the sight, but there was no time for hesitation. They had to act, and they had to act fast.

Charles was the first to reach her, dropping to his knees as he cut through the ropes with the crowbar. Emma's eyes filled with tears as the gag was removed, her body trembling with fear and cold.

"Are you okay?" Clara asked, her voice choked with emotion as she knelt beside Emma.

Emma nodded weakly, her voice barely above a whisper. "They... they were going to kill me..."

"But they didn't," Clara said firmly, her hand gripping Emma's tightly. "You're safe now. We've got you."

The relief was palpable, but it was short-lived. As they helped Emma to her feet, Clara couldn't shake the feeling that they were still being watched, that their enemies were still out there, waiting for the right moment to strike.

"We need to get back to the inn," Charles said urgently, his eyes scanning the darkness around them. "We're not safe out here."

The group quickly made their way back through the woods, Emma leaning heavily on Clara as they trudged through the snow. The forest seemed even darker now, the shadows longer and more menacing. But they didn't stop, didn't slow down. They had found Emma, and now they had to get her to safety.

As they approached the inn, Clara's heart pounded in her chest. The lights from the building cast a faint glow across the snow, a beacon in the darkness. But the sense of unease didn't fade. Something was still out there, something dangerous, and Clara knew they couldn't let their guard down.

They reached the inn, the warmth of the interior a stark contrast to the cold and fear outside. But even as they barricaded the doors and windows once more, even as they settled Emma by the fire and tried to calm their racing hearts, Clara couldn't shake the feeling that this was far from over.

The attacker had been just one piece of the puzzle, one threat among many. And as Clara looked into the darkened corners of the room, the flickering shadows cast by the fire, she knew that the real danger was still out there, waiting.

But they had survived. They had found Emma. And they were still together. That had to count for something.

As the night wore on, the group huddled together, their resolve hardening. They had faced down one threat, and they would face down whatever came next.

14

Chapter 14

The warmth of the inn's interior was a fleeting comfort as Clara and the others huddled together around Emma, trying to catch their breath after the frantic search through the woods. The relief of having found Emma, of having brought her back safely, was palpable—but it was quickly overshadowed by a creeping realization that they were still far from safe.

Emma shivered as she sat by the fire, her face pale and her body trembling despite the blankets they had wrapped around her. The fear in her eyes was raw, and Clara felt a pang of guilt for not being able to protect her better. But they had to focus on what was ahead, on what they needed to do to keep everyone safe.

"Are you feeling any better?" Clara asked softly, kneeling beside Emma and gently rubbing her back.

Emma nodded, though her voice was still shaky. "I—I'm okay. Just… I was so scared. I thought they were going to…"

Clara squeezed her hand, her own fear bubbling just beneath the surface. "You're safe now. We're all here, and we won't let anything happen to you."

But even as she said the words, Clara couldn't shake the feeling that something was terribly wrong. The whole night had been one long, unrelenting nightmare, and though they had survived the immediate threat, the danger was far from over.

Charles, who had been pacing near the window, suddenly stopped and turned to the group, his expression dark and troubled. "Something's not right," he said, his voice low and filled with suspicion. "The whole thing—the attack, Emma's kidnapping—it all feels too… orchestrated."

Clara frowned, the unease in her chest growing. "What do you mean?"

"Think about it," Charles replied, his brow furrowed. "That man broke in, and while we were distracted fighting him off, Emma was taken. It's like they knew exactly how we'd react, like they were planning it all along."

Clara's heart sank as the implications of Charles's words hit her. The attack, the kidnapping, the frantic search in the woods—it had all been a setup. A way to manipulate them, to keep them off balance, while their enemies moved the pieces into place.

"They're playing with us," Daniel said, his voice tight with frustration. "They're making us jump through hoops, and we're falling for it every time."

Sarah looked around the room, her eyes wide with worry. "But why? What's the endgame here? What do they want?"

Before anyone could answer, Margaret, who had been sitting quietly by the fire, suddenly stood up, her eyes filled with alarm. "Our things," she said, her voice trembling. "They took our things."

Clara's heart skipped a beat as she realized what Margaret meant. In their rush to find Emma, they had left all their belongings behind—wallets, phones, supplies, everything. And now, the realization hit them all at once: they had been robbed.

They quickly spread out through the inn, checking every room, every nook and cranny where they had left their belongings. But it was all gone. Every last item of value had been taken, leaving them with nothing but the clothes on their backs and the few makeshift weapons they had managed to hold onto.

Clara's pulse quickened as she rummaged through the empty drawers, her mind racing with the enormity of what had just happened. They had been set up from the start, led into a trap while their enemies stripped them of everything they had. It was a crushing blow, one that left them feeling vulnerable and exposed in a way they hadn't felt before.

"They took everything," Emma said, her voice barely above a whisper as she stood in the doorway, her face pale with shock. "How did they do it so quickly?"

"They were watching us," Charles said grimly, his jaw clenched as he stared at the empty space where his belongings had been. "They knew exactly when we left the inn, and they knew exactly how much time they had to get in and out. This was planned down to the last detail."

Daniel kicked at a nearby chair, his frustration boiling over. "Damn it! We're being played like puppets! They're running circles around us, and we're just reacting to everything they throw at us."

Clara felt a wave of helplessness wash over her. They were trapped, isolated, and now they had nothing left—no way to call for help, no supplies, no sense of security. The enemy was outmaneuvering them at every turn, and it was becoming increasingly clear that they were losing this battle.

"They're winning," Margaret said quietly, her voice filled with despair. "They're winning, and we're just… we're just…"

"No," Clara interrupted, her voice firm despite the despair clawing at her insides. "We can't think like that. We can't give up. That's exactly what they want—for us to feel defeated, to lose hope."

"But how can we fight back?" Sarah asked, her voice trembling with fear. "We have nothing left. They've taken everything."

"We still have each other," Clara replied, her gaze sweeping over the group. "We're still here, and as long as we stick together, we have a chance. We just need to be smarter, to think ahead."

Charles nodded, his expression hardening as he considered Clara's words. "She's right. We can't let them keep playing us. We need to get ahead of them, figure out what their next move is and be ready for it."

"But how?" Emma asked, her voice small and uncertain. "We don't even know who they are or what they want."

"We start by looking at what we do know," Clara said, trying to inject some confidence into her voice. "They've been watching us, manipulating us. They're using fear to control us, to make us react instead of think. But we can turn that around. We can start playing their game, make them react to us."

"How?" Daniel asked, his frustration still evident, but with a spark of curiosity.

Clara paused, thinking hard. She knew they were up against a formidable opponent, someone who was always a step ahead. But they had to try something different, something unexpected.

They couldn't keep playing by their enemy's rules.

"We set a trap," Clara said finally, her voice steady with resolve. "We make them think we're panicking, that we're falling apart. But instead, we'll be ready for them."

Charles looked at her with renewed interest. "What kind of trap?"

Clara's mind raced as she pieced together a plan. "They've been relying on our fear, our need to protect ourselves, to control the situation. But if we make them think they've won, that we're broken… they might get careless. We'll lure them in, make them come to us. And when they do, we'll be ready."

"But what if they don't fall for it?" Margaret asked, her voice laced with doubt.

Clara met her gaze, her expression firm. "Then we'll come up with something else. But we have to try. We can't just sit here and wait for them to finish us off."

The group was silent for a moment, each of them weighing Clara's words. The situation was dire, and the odds were stacked against them. But the alternative—doing nothing, continuing to let their enemies dictate the terms—was even worse.

Charles nodded slowly, his resolve hardening. "Alright. Let's do it. We'll make them think we're defeated, that we're not a threat anymore. And when they come for us, we'll turn the tables."

The others agreed, though Clara could see the uncertainty in their eyes. They were all scared, all feeling the weight of their situation pressing down on them. But they were also determined. Determined not to let their enemies win without a fight.

They spent the next hour carefully preparing the inn for

their trap. They left certain doors and windows unblocked, creating the illusion that they were losing control, that they were too panicked to properly secure their surroundings. They scattered a few items around, making it look like they had hastily abandoned them in a state of desperation. Everything was designed to send a message: that the group inside the inn was scared, disorganized, and vulnerable.

But behind the scenes, they were anything but. They armed themselves with whatever makeshift weapons they could find—crowbars, kitchen knives, heavy objects that could be used as bludgeons. They set up positions around the inn where they could remain hidden but still have a clear view of the entrances. If the intruders came for them again, they wouldn't be caught off guard this time.

As they worked, Clara couldn't shake the nagging feeling that they were missing something, that the intruders had more tricks up their sleeves. But she pushed the thoughts aside. They couldn't afford to second-guess themselves now. They had to commit to the plan and see it through.

By the time they were finished, the inn looked like a scene of chaos—furniture overturned, belongings strewn about, doors and windows left partially open. But beneath the surface, the group was focused and ready. They took their positions, hiding in the shadows, their hearts pounding as they waited for the intruders to take the bait.

The minutes stretched into hours, the tension thickening with each passing moment. The wind howled outside, rattling the windows and adding to the oppressive atmosphere. Clara crouched behind an overturned sofa, her grip tight on the kitchen knife she had chosen as her weapon. Her eyes darted around the room, scanning for any sign of movement, any hint that their enemies had taken the bait.

Then she heard it—a faint creak, the sound of a door being pushed open. Her pulse quickened as she strained to listen, her breath catching in her throat. The creak was followed by the soft shuffle of footsteps, barely audible over the howling wind. Someone was inside the inn.

Clara's heart raced as she tightened her grip on the knife, her muscles tense and ready to spring into action. She could hear the intruder moving through the inn, their steps cautious but confident. They thought they had won, that they were walking into a situation where their prey was broken and defeated. But they were wrong.

The footsteps grew closer, the sound echoing through the empty halls of the inn. Clara held her breath, waiting for the signal, waiting for the moment when they would strike. The tension was almost unbearable, each second stretching on like an eternity.

Then, just as the intruder reached the edge of the room, Clara heard a loud crash from the other side of the inn—someone had knocked over a piece of furniture, creating a diversion. The intruder paused, clearly startled by the noise, and in that moment of hesitation, Charles sprang into action.

With a shout, Charles lunged at the intruder, the crowbar swinging with deadly precision. The man barely had time to react before the metal connected with his head, sending him crashing to the floor. The force of the blow was enough to knock him out cold, his body crumpling in a heap.

"Now!" Charles shouted, his voice filled with urgency.

The rest of the group emerged from their hiding spots, moving quickly to secure the intruder. Daniel and Margaret bound his hands and feet with whatever they could find, ensuring that he wouldn't be able to escape or fight back when he regained consciousness.

Clara's heart pounded in her chest as she stared down at the man lying on the floor. He was dressed in dark clothing, just like the previous attacker, his face obscured by a balaclava. But now that they had him, they could finally get some answers—find out who he was, who he was working for, and what they wanted.

Charles knelt beside the man, pulling off the balaclava to reveal a rugged, unshaven face. The man groaned, his eyes fluttering open as he slowly regained consciousness. He blinked, disoriented, before realizing the situation he was in. His eyes narrowed with anger and fear as he struggled against his bindings.

"Who are you?" Charles demanded, his voice cold and hard. "Who are you working for?"

The man didn't answer, his lips pressed into a thin line. Clara could see the defiance in his eyes, the determination not to give them anything. But they didn't have time for games.

"We're not going to ask again," Clara said, stepping forward, her voice steady despite the adrenaline surging through her veins. "Who sent you? What do you want from us?"

The man's gaze flicked from Clara to the others, his expression unreadable. For a moment, Clara thought he might actually answer, but then his eyes hardened, and he spat on the floor, his defiance clear.

"Go to hell," he muttered, his voice dripping with contempt.

Charles's jaw tightened, his grip on the crowbar tightening. But before he could say anything else, a loud crash echoed through the inn—this time from the direction of the kitchen. The group tensed, their eyes widening in alarm.

"What was that?" Margaret asked, her voice filled with dread.

Before anyone could answer, another crash followed, this one closer, louder. It sounded like something—or someone—was breaking through the barricades they had set up earlier. Clara's heart raced as she realized what was happening.

"It's a diversion," she said, her voice filled with urgency. "There's more of them—they're trying to get in!"

Charles and Daniel quickly moved to secure the room, but it was too late. The door to the kitchen burst open, and two more intruders stormed in, their faces obscured by balaclavas, their movements swift and ruthless.

Clara barely had time to react before one of the intruders grabbed her from behind, his grip like iron as he twisted her arm, forcing her to drop the knife. She struggled against him, her breath coming in short, panicked gasps as she tried to break free.

"Let her go!" Charles shouted, charging at the intruder with the crowbar raised.

But the other intruder was quicker, catching Charles off guard and knocking the crowbar out of his hand with a swift kick. Charles stumbled, but quickly regained his footing, his eyes blazing with determination as he faced off against the attackers.

Clara fought with everything she had, using her free hand to claw at the intruder's face, but his grip only tightened, his strength overpowering her. She could feel the panic rising in her chest, but she refused to give in. She had to keep fighting, had to find a way out.

Suddenly, the intruder holding her released his grip, shoving her away with a force that sent her crashing into the wall. Clara's head spun, pain flaring in her side as she struggled to stay upright. She looked up, dazed, just in time to see Charles tackle one of the intruders to the ground, the two of them grappling for control.

The other intruder moved toward the bound man on the floor, clearly intending to free him. But before he could reach him, Daniel lunged at him, knocking him off balance and sending him crashing into a nearby table.

The room erupted into chaos, the sounds of the struggle filling the air as the group fought with everything they had. Clara pushed herself to her feet, her vision swimming as she grabbed a nearby chair and swung it at the intruder who had grabbed her earlier.

The chair connected with a satisfying thud, and the intruder staggered, momentarily disoriented. But it wasn't enough to bring him down. He quickly recovered, turning on Clara with a snarl, his fists clenched.

Clara braced herself, ready to fight with everything she had left. But before the intruder could reach her, Charles appeared at her side, swinging the crowbar with all his strength. The metal connected with the intruder's head, sending him crashing to the floor, unconscious.

"Are you okay?" Charles asked, his voice filled with concern as he helped Clara steady herself.

Clara nodded, though her heart was still racing. "Yeah. I'm okay. Thanks."

The remaining intruder, seeing that the odds had turned against him, quickly backed away, his eyes darting between Charles and Daniel, who were both armed and ready to strike. For a moment, it looked like he might try to make a run for it, but then he raised his hands in surrender, his face hidden behind the balaclava.

Charles didn't hesitate. He moved forward, grabbing the intruder by the collar and forcing him to the ground. Daniel quickly bound the man's hands, ensuring that he wouldn't be able to fight back.

The room fell into a tense silence, the aftermath of the struggle hanging heavily in the air. Clara's breath came in ragged gasps as she surveyed the scene. The attackers were subdued, but the victory felt hollow. They had been set up, manipulated into letting their guard down, and though they had fought back, the realization that their enemies were still one step ahead was hard to shake.

"They were trying to distract us," Charles said, his voice filled with frustration as he knelt beside the bound man on the floor. "This whole thing—it was all a setup."

"They knew we'd go after Emma," Clara said, her voice filled with bitterness. "They wanted us to leave the inn so they could get inside, so they could take everything."

"They're winning," Margaret said quietly, her voice filled with despair. "They're winning, and we're just playing into their hands."

Clara wanted to deny it, to find some silver lining in the situation, but she couldn't. The truth was staring them in the face, undeniable and terrifying. They were being outmaneuvered at every turn, and their enemies were winning the game.

But as Clara looked around the room, at the bound intruders and the determination in her friends' eyes, she knew they couldn't give up. They had come this far, and they had to keep fighting, no matter how desperate the situation seemed.

"We're not done yet," Clara said firmly, her voice filled with resolve. "We've survived this long, and we'll keep surviving.

We just need to be smarter, to stay one step ahead of them."

"But how?" Daniel asked, his voice filled with frustration. "How do we beat them when they're always ahead of us?"

Clara didn't have an answer, not yet. But she knew they had to keep trying, had to find a way to turn the tables. The game wasn't over, and as long as they were still standing, there was still a chance.

"We'll figure it out," Clara said, her voice steady. "We'll find a way to beat them."

Charles nodded, his expression hardening with determination. "We have to."

The group exchanged tense glances, each of them feeling the weight of the situation pressing down on them. They had been set up, manipulated, and stripped of everything they had, but they were still alive, still together. And as long as they had each other, they had a fighting chance.

The night was far from over, and the battle was only just beginning. But Clara knew they had to keep going, had to keep fighting, no matter what it took. The storm outside was nothing compared to the storm within the inn, but they would face it head-on, together.

As the wind howled outside, rattling the windows and filling the air with a sense of foreboding, Clara steeled herself for whatever came next. The game was far from over, and the stakes had never been higher. But she was determined to see it through to the end—no matter what the cost.

15

Chapter 15

The room was eerily quiet after the struggle, the only sounds the labored breathing of the group and the faint crackle of the fire. The adrenaline from the fight was starting to wear off, leaving Clara with a deep exhaustion that seemed to settle into her bones. She stared at the bound intruders, their faces obscured by balaclavas, and felt a chill that had nothing to do with the cold outside. They had won this round, but the victory felt hollow. They were still in danger, still at the mercy of an enemy who seemed always one step ahead.

Charles was the first to break the silence, his voice low and steady. "We need to figure out what to do with these guys. We can't just leave them here."

Daniel nodded, his face set in a grim line. "We should tie them up somewhere more secure, maybe one of the storage rooms. We'll deal with them when we've figured out our next move."

Margaret, still shaken from the fight, moved toward the kitchen, her hands trembling. "I'll get some rope or something.

We need to make sure they can't get loose."

Clara stood up, her legs feeling weak beneath her. The shock of everything that had happened was beginning to set in, but she pushed it down, focusing on the task at hand. "I'll help," she said, moving to follow Margaret. But before she could take more than a few steps, the lights flickered.

Everyone froze, their eyes snapping to the ceiling as the overhead lights flickered again, dimming to a faint glow before finally going out completely. The room was plunged into darkness, broken only by the dim light of the fire.

"What the hell?" Daniel muttered, his voice tense.

"The generator," Charles said, his tone grim. "It's gone out."

Clara's heart sank. The generator had been their lifeline, the only thing keeping the inn warm and lit in the middle of the snowstorm. Without it, they were left in the dark, with no power, no heat, and no way to contact the outside world.

Margaret's voice trembled as she spoke. "What do we do? We can't stay here in the dark. It's too dangerous."

Charles didn't hesitate. "We need to get more fuel for the generator. There should be some extra cans in the shed. If we can find enough, we might be able to get it running again."

"But what if there isn't enough?" Emma asked, her voice small and filled with worry. "What if we can't get it started?"

Charles's jaw tightened. "Then we'll have to find another way. But first, we need to check the shed. We can't just sit here and hope for the best."

Clara nodded, though the thought of venturing out into the cold, dark night filled her with dread. But they had no choice. They couldn't stay in the inn without power, not with the threat of more intruders looming over them.

"Let's go," she said, trying to inject some confidence into

her voice. "The sooner we check the shed, the sooner we can figure out what to do next."

The group quickly gathered what they needed—flashlights, heavy coats, and anything that could be used as a weapon. The fear of what might be waiting for them outside was a constant presence, but they pushed it aside, focusing on the task ahead.

As they stepped outside, the cold air hit them like a wall, the wind biting at their exposed skin. The snow was still falling, a steady, relentless blanket that covered everything in a thick layer of white. The darkness was oppressive, the sky a deep, inky black that seemed to swallow up the faint light from their flashlights.

Clara's breath came in short, sharp gasps as they trudged through the snow, the cold seeping into her bones. The fear of what might be out there, lurking in the darkness, gnawed at her, but she forced herself to stay focused. They had a job to do, and they couldn't afford to let their imaginations get the better of them.

The shed loomed ahead, a dark, hulking shape against the snow-covered landscape. Charles was the first to reach it, his breath visible in the cold air as he pushed the door open. The hinges creaked loudly in the stillness, and the group's flashlights cast long, twisted shadows on the walls as they stepped inside.

The shed was filled with old tools, gardening supplies, and other odds and ends, all covered in a thick layer of dust. The snowmobile sat in the corner, untouched and unused, its once-bright paint dulled by time.

"There should be some gas cans around here," Charles said, his voice low as he scanned the shelves. "Start looking."

Clara moved to the back of the shed, her flashlight sweeping over the cluttered shelves. The cold was even more pronounced inside the shed, the wind whistling through the gaps in the walls and chilling her to the bone. But she pushed the discomfort aside, focusing on the task at hand.

After a few minutes of searching, Daniel let out a frustrated sigh. "There's nothing here. Just empty cans."

Clara's heart sank, the reality of their situation beginning to set in. If they couldn't find any fuel, they were stuck in the dark, with no way to power the generator and no way to keep the inn warm. And in the middle of a snowstorm, that could be a death sentence.

"Keep looking," Charles said, his tone filled with urgency. "There has to be something."

Margaret, who had been searching near the snowmobile, suddenly spoke up. "I found something!" She held up a small gas can, its red paint chipped and faded. "There's not much, but it might be enough to get the snowmobile started."

Clara felt a flicker of hope. It wasn't enough to power the generator, but if they could get the snowmobile running, they could send someone for help. It was a long shot, but it was better than sitting in the dark, waiting for something—or someone—to come for them.

"We can try it," Clara said, her voice filled with determination. "It's our best option right now."

Charles nodded, already moving toward the snowmobile. "Let's get it fueled up. If we can get it started, I'll go for help."

The group quickly gathered around the snowmobile as Charles unscrewed the gas cap and carefully poured the contents of the small can into the tank. The fuel level barely budged, but it was better than nothing. It might be enough to get Charles to the nearest town, where he could find help and bring back supplies.

Once the tank was filled, Charles checked the snowmobile's engine, his brow furrowed in concentration. "It hasn't been used in a long time," he muttered, more to himself than to the others. "But it should still run."

Clara watched anxiously as Charles primed the engine, then pulled the starter cord with a firm, practiced motion. The engine sputtered, coughing to life for a brief moment before dying again. He tried a second time, and then a third, each attempt met with the same frustrating result.

"Come on," Charles muttered, his voice filled with tension as he pulled the cord again.

The engine sputtered once more, then roared to life, the sound loud and harsh in the stillness of the night. Clara let out a breath she hadn't realized she was holding, a wave of relief washing over her. They had done it. They had a way out.

"It's running," Charles said, his voice filled with a mix of relief and determination. "I'll take the snowmobile to the nearest town and get help. It's a long shot, but it's our best chance."

Clara felt a surge of gratitude for Charles's bravery. He was willing to risk everything to get them the help they needed, to keep them safe. But the thought of him out there, alone in the snowstorm, filled her with worry.

"Be careful," she said, her voice soft but firm. "We're counting on you."

Charles nodded, his expression serious. "I'll be back as soon as I can. Just… stay safe, all of you. Keep the fire going, and don't let anyone in unless you're sure it's me."

The group exchanged tense glances, each of them feeling the weight of the situation pressing down on them. Charles was their best chance, but they all knew how dangerous it was out there, how slim the odds were.

Charles mounted the snowmobile, his movements confident despite the uncertainty of what lay ahead. The engine roared as he revved it, the sound filling the air as he prepared to leave.

"Good luck," Daniel said, his voice filled with a mixture of hope and fear.

Charles gave them one last nod, then kicked the snowmobile into gear, the tracks biting into the snow as he sped off into the night. The sound of the engine quickly faded into the distance, swallowed up by the wind and snow, leaving the group standing in the cold, dark shed, feeling more isolated than ever.

For a moment, no one spoke. The weight of the decision they had just made, the uncertainty of what would happen next, hung heavily in the air. Clara felt a knot of anxiety tighten in her chest, but she forced herself to stay calm. They had done the right thing. They had to believe that Charles would make it, that he would bring back help.

"We should get back inside," Clara said finally, breaking the silence. "We need to keep the fire going, and we need to stay together."

The group nodded, their faces filled with a mixture of exhaustion and determination. They had no choice but to keep going, to hold on to the hope that Charles would return with help.

As they made their way back to the inn, the cold seemed even more biting, the darkness more oppressive. The snow crunched under their boots, the sound loud in the otherwise silent night. Clara's breath came in short, sharp puffs, the cold air burning in her lungs.

When they reached the inn, the warmth of the fire was a

welcome relief, but it did little to chase away the unease that had settled over them. The shadows cast by the flickering flames seemed to dance on the walls, twisting into ominous shapes that only heightened their sense of vulnerability.

They quickly set about making the inn as secure as possible, double-checking the barricades and making sure that the intruders they had subdued were still tightly bound. The fear of another attack, of being caught off guard again, was a constant presence, but they did their best to push it aside.

Margaret moved to the fireplace, carefully adding more wood to the flames. The fire crackled and hissed, the warmth spreading through the room, but the darkness beyond the flickering light seemed to press in on them from all sides.

"We need to keep the fire going," Margaret said quietly, her voice trembling slightly. "It's the only thing keeping us warm."

"And the only thing giving us any light," Emma added, her voice barely above a whisper.

Clara nodded, though the flickering firelight did little to ease her nerves. The darkness outside the circle of light felt alive, as if it were watching them, waiting for the right moment to strike. The isolation, the uncertainty of what lay beyond the walls of the inn, was almost suffocating.

But they had to keep going. They had to believe that Charles would make it, that he would return with help before it was too late.

They settled into an uneasy silence, the only sounds the crackling of the fire and the occasional creak of the old wooden floorboards. The cold seemed to seep into their bones, the darkness pressing in on them, but they stayed close to the fire, drawing what little comfort they could from its warmth.

Hours passed, the night dragging on with agonizing slowness. The fear of what might come next was a constant presence, gnawing at the edges of Clara's mind, but she refused to let it consume her. They had made it this far, and they would make it through the night.

But as the hours stretched on, Clara couldn't shake the feeling that something was wrong. The inn was too quiet, too still, as if it were holding its breath, waiting for something to happen. The wind howled outside, the windows rattling in their frames, but inside, there was only the crackling of the fire and the tense, heavy silence.

Then, just as Clara was beginning to think that the night might pass without incident, she heard it—a faint sound, barely audible over the wind. It was a soft, scraping noise, like something brushing against the walls of the inn.

Her heart skipped a beat, her pulse quickening as she strained to listen. The sound came again, closer this time, more distinct. It was coming from outside, near the back of the inn.

"Did you hear that?" Clara whispered, her voice trembling.

The others looked up, their eyes wide with fear as they listened. The sound came again, louder now, more insistent. It was a deliberate, methodical scraping, as if someone—or something—was trying to get in.

"We need to check it out," Daniel said, his voice tight with tension.

Clara nodded, though the thought of going outside, of facing whatever was making that noise, filled her with dread. But they couldn't just sit there, waiting for it to find a way in. They had to be proactive, had to take control.

"We'll go together," Clara said, her voice steadier than she felt. "Margaret and Emma, stay here and keep the fire going. Daniel and I will check it out."

Charles wasn't there to lead them anymore, and Clara felt the weight of responsibility settle on her shoulders. They needed to be smart, to stay calm, and to keep each other safe.

Margaret and Emma nodded, their faces pale but determined. "Be careful," Margaret said, her voice barely above a whisper.

Clara and Daniel exchanged a tense glance, then moved toward the back door. The cold air hit them like a wall as they stepped outside, the wind whipping around them, carrying with it the promise of danger. The sound was louder now, closer, and Clara's heart pounded in her chest as they moved cautiously toward the source.

The snow crunched under their boots, the darkness pressing in on them as they rounded the corner of the inn. Clara held her breath, her eyes straining to see through the gloom. The sound was coming from just ahead, near the rear wall of the inn.

Daniel signaled for Clara to stay back, and she nodded, gripping the handle of the kitchen knife she had brought with her. The cold metal was reassuring in her hand, a small comfort in the face of the unknown.

Daniel moved forward, his steps careful and deliberate as he approached the source of the noise. Clara's breath caught in her throat, her heart pounding as she watched him disappear around the corner.

There was a moment of tense silence, broken only by the howling wind. Then, suddenly, Daniel called out, his voice filled with a mixture of relief and frustration.

"It's just a branch," he said, his voice carrying over the wind. "A tree branch broke off and is scraping against the wall."

Clara let out a breath she hadn't realized she was holding,

the tension in her chest easing slightly. It wasn't an intruder, just a fallen branch. But the relief was short-lived. The night was far from over, and they were still in danger.

Daniel returned, his face flushed from the cold. "It's fine," he said, his voice low as he glanced around the darkened landscape. "But we need to stay on our guard. There could be more out there."

Clara nodded, her heart still racing. "Let's get back inside. We need to stay close to the fire."

They quickly made their way back to the inn, the cold air biting at their skin. The wind howled around them, the darkness pressing in, but they stayed close, drawing strength from each other.

When they reached the inn, the warmth of the fire was a welcome relief, but the fear of what might come next lingered. They had made it through another night, but the battle was far from over.

As they settled back by the fire, Clara couldn't shake the feeling that they were running out of time. Charles was out there, somewhere, fighting his way through the storm to bring back help. But the night was long, and the dangers were many. They had to hold on, had to survive until he returned.

The shadows danced on the walls, twisting into ominous shapes as the fire crackled in the hearth. The wind rattled the windows, and the darkness outside felt more oppressive than ever. But they were still together, still fighting.

And as long as they had each other, there was hope.

16

Chapter 16

The night stretched on, the minutes crawling by with agonizing slowness. The fire in the hearth had burned down to a dim glow, the wood reduced to smoldering embers that barely cast any light. Clara sat with her back against the wall, her knees drawn up to her chest, trying to ward off the cold that seemed to seep into every corner of the room. The wind outside continued its relentless assault on the inn, rattling the windows and filling the air with a low, mournful howl.

Emma and Margaret huddled together on the sofa, their faces drawn and pale. They had barely spoken since returning from the shed, the fear and uncertainty hanging over them like a shroud. Daniel was pacing near the door, his movements restless and agitated, as if he couldn't bear to sit still for another moment. The tension in the room was thick, almost suffocating, and it was clear that everyone was on edge, their nerves frayed from the constant strain of the past few days.

Clara's thoughts kept drifting back to Charles. She pictured him out there in the snow, fighting his way through the storm on the snowmobile, the cold biting at his skin and the wind whipping around him. The odds were against him, and she knew it. But she had to believe that he would make it, that he would find help and bring it back before it was too late.

But even as she clung to that hope, a nagging doubt gnawed at the edges of her mind. What if he didn't make it? What if the snowmobile broke down, or he got lost in the storm? What if…?

She pushed the thoughts away, refusing to give in to the fear. They had come this far, and they had to keep going. They had to survive.

The silence in the room was oppressive, the only sounds the occasional crackle of the fire and the relentless wind outside. Clara's eyes kept drifting to the windows, half-expecting to see a shadowy figure lurking outside, waiting for the right moment to strike. But there was nothing—just the endless darkness, broken only by the faint glow of the embers.

"We need to keep the fire going," Margaret said quietly, her voice trembling as she broke the silence. "It's getting colder."

Clara nodded, though she knew that the small pile of wood they had left wouldn't last much longer. The generator was out, and with it, their only reliable source of heat. If the fire went out, they would be left in the dark, with nothing but the cold to keep them company.

"I'll get more wood," Daniel offered, his voice tight with tension. "We can't let the fire die."

Clara watched as Daniel moved to the small stack of logs they had gathered earlier, his movements quick and efficient. He added a few more pieces to the fire, the flames flickering to life for a brief moment before settling back into a steady, if weak, glow.

As the fire crackled softly, Clara's mind kept returning to the events of the night. The intruders, the attack, the realization that they were being watched and manipulated. It was all part of some twisted game, a game they were losing. The thought of it made her stomach turn, but she knew they couldn't afford to dwell on it. They had to stay focused, had to keep fighting.

"What do you think they want?" Emma asked suddenly, her voice small and filled with uncertainty. "Why are they doing this to us?"

Clara didn't have an answer, and she could see the same confusion and fear mirrored in the faces of the others. It was a question that had been gnawing at them all, but one they had no way of answering. The intruders had been relentless, their attacks calculated and precise, but their motives remained a mystery.

"Maybe it's not about what they want," Daniel said, his voice tinged with bitterness as he stared into the fire. "Maybe they're just doing it because they can. Because they want to see how far they can push us before we break."

Margaret shuddered, her eyes wide with fear. "But why us? Why this place?"

Clara shook her head, her thoughts racing. "I don't know. But we can't let them break us. We have to stay strong, no matter what they throw at us."

Emma hugged her knees to her chest, her voice trembling as she spoke. "What if we can't? What if this is too much for us?"

Clara looked at Emma, seeing the fear and doubt in her eyes, and felt a pang of sympathy. They were all feeling the strain, all struggling to hold on to hope in the face of overwhelming odds. But she knew that they couldn't afford to give in to despair. Not now, not when they were so close to the end.

"We can't think like that," Clara said firmly, her voice steady despite the turmoil inside her. "We've made it this far because we've stayed together, because we haven't given up. And we can't start giving up now."

Daniel stopped pacing, his eyes narrowing as he looked at Clara. "What if they're not just trying to scare us? What if there's something here that they want? Something they're trying to get?"

The question hung in the air, heavy with implications. It was a thought that had crossed Clara's mind before, but she hadn't wanted to dwell on it. The idea that there was some hidden motive behind the attacks, some unknown prize that the intruders were after, was almost too terrifying to consider.

But as she thought about it, the pieces began to fall into place. The intruders had been methodical in their actions, targeting specific areas of the inn, driving them out of certain rooms, and taking their belongings. It wasn't just random violence—it was deliberate, calculated.

"There must be something here," Clara said slowly, her mind racing as she tried to piece it all together. "Something they want, something they're willing to do anything to get."

Margaret's face went pale, her eyes wide with realization. "But what? What could possibly be worth all of this?"

Clara didn't have an answer, but she knew they had to figure it out. If they could understand what the intruders were after, they might be able to find a way to stop them, to turn the tables and regain control.

"We need to search the inn," Clara said, her voice filled with determination. "There has to be something here, something we've missed. If we can find it, maybe we can use it against them."

Daniel nodded, his expression serious. "We'll search every room, every corner. If there's something here, we'll find it."

Emma looked hesitant, her fear evident in her eyes. "But what if we find it? What if it's something… dangerous?"

Clara met Emma's gaze, her own resolve hardening. "Then we'll deal with it. But we can't keep running, can't keep hiding. We have to take control, or they'll keep coming for us."

The group exchanged tense glances, each of them weighing the risks and the unknowns. It was a dangerous plan, one that could lead them deeper into the intruders' trap, but they had no other choice. They couldn't afford to sit and wait for the next attack, not when their enemies were winning the game.

They decided to split up, each of them taking a section of the inn to search. Clara and Daniel would start with the basement, while Emma and Margaret would search the upper floors. It was a risky move, especially with the power out, but they couldn't waste any more time.

As they prepared to head out, Clara grabbed one of the remaining flashlights, her hand trembling slightly as she turned it on. The beam of light cut through the darkness, but it was weak, barely enough to light the way.

"Stay close," Clara said, her voice steady despite the anxiety gnawing at her. "We need to be careful. We don't know what we're dealing with."

Daniel nodded, his own flashlight held tightly in his hand. "We'll find it, whatever it is. We have to."

With that, they set off, the group splitting up and heading in different directions. The inn was eerily silent, the darkness oppressive as they moved through the narrow hallways, their footsteps muffled by the thick carpet. Clara's heart pounded in her chest, her pulse quickening as they descended the creaking wooden stairs into the basement.

The basement was even colder than the rest of the inn, the air damp and musty. Clara's flashlight beam flickered as she swept it across the walls, revealing rows of old, dusty shelves lined with forgotten tools and boxes. The stone walls were rough and uninviting, adding to the sense of foreboding that seemed to hang in the air.

Daniel followed closely behind her, his own flashlight cutting through the darkness as he examined the floor and corners for any sign of what they were looking for. The basement seemed to go on forever, a labyrinth of narrow passageways and low ceilings, all of it feeling more oppressive with each step they took.

"What exactly are we hoping to find down here?" Daniel asked, his voice low and cautious.

Clara shook her head, though she knew he couldn't see the gesture in the dim light. "I'm not sure," she admitted. "But if there's something here that they want, it could be hidden down here. We need to check everything."

Daniel nodded, his expression grim as he continued to search. The basement was filled with old, forgotten items—rusty tools, broken furniture, boxes of yellowed papers. It seemed unlikely that anything of value could be hidden in such a place, but Clara knew they couldn't afford to overlook anything.

As they moved deeper into the basement, the air grew colder, the darkness thicker. The sound of their footsteps echoed off the stone walls, creating a hollow, unsettling noise that set Clara's nerves on edge. The fear that had been gnawing at her all night seemed to intensify with each step they took, but she forced herself to stay focused. They had to find something—

anything—that could explain why they were being targeted.

Suddenly, Daniel stopped, his flashlight beam focused on a section of the wall that looked different from the rest. "Clara, come look at this."

Clara hurried over, her flashlight joining Daniel's as they examined the wall. It was made of the same rough stone as the rest of the basement, but there was something odd about it—a faint outline, barely visible, that suggested there might be a hidden door or compartment.

"Do you think this could be it?" Daniel asked, his voice filled with a mix of excitement and apprehension.

Clara's heart raced as she ran her fingers along the outline, feeling for any signs of a hidden latch or handle. The stone was cold and rough under her fingertips, but she could feel a slight give, as if the wall wasn't as solid as it appeared.

"It could be," she said, her voice trembling with a mixture of fear and anticipation. "Help me push on it."

Together, they pressed against the stone, using their combined strength to try and move it. For a moment, nothing happened, and Clara began to wonder if they were wasting their time. But then, with a low groan, the stone began to shift, sliding inward with a heavy, grinding sound.

Clara and Daniel exchanged a tense glance as the hidden door revealed a narrow passageway beyond, barely wide enough for a person to squeeze through. The air that wafted out was colder still, carrying with it a damp, earthy smell that made Clara's skin crawl.

"We should check it out," Daniel said, his voice steady despite the unease in his eyes.

Clara nodded, though the thought of what might be lurking in the darkness beyond the passageway filled her with dread.

But they had come this far, and they couldn't turn back now.

They squeezed through the narrow opening, their flashlights barely illuminating the cramped space. The passageway was lined with old wooden beams, some of them rotting and crumbling with age. The floor was uneven, the stone slick with moisture, and Clara had to be careful not to lose her footing.

The passageway twisted and turned, leading them deeper into the bowels of the inn. Clara's heart pounded in her chest, her breath coming in short, sharp gasps as the walls seemed to close in around them. The fear that had been gnawing at her all night was now a constant presence, but she pushed it aside, focusing on the light from her flashlight and the path ahead.

After what felt like an eternity, the passageway opened up into a small chamber. The air was stale, and the walls were lined with shelves, each one filled with old, decaying books and strange, unidentifiable objects. At the far end of the chamber was a large wooden chest, its surface covered in a thick layer of dust.

Clara's flashlight beam settled on the chest, and she felt a shiver run down her spine. There was something ominous about it, something that made her want to turn around and leave the chamber as quickly as possible. But she knew they had to see what was inside.

Daniel moved forward, his flashlight illuminating the chest as he reached out to open it. The wood creaked as the lid lifted, revealing the contents inside.

Clara stepped closer, her heart pounding as she peered into the chest. Inside, nestled among layers of old, rotting fabric, was a collection of strange, ancient-looking objects. There were small, intricately carved statues, old parchment scrolls, and a large, ornate key made of a dark, heavy metal.

"What is all this?" Daniel asked, his voice filled with awe and confusion.

Clara shook her head, her mind racing as she tried to make sense of what they were seeing. "I don't know… but this must be what they're after."

She reached into the chest, her fingers brushing against the cold metal of the key. There was something about it that drew her in, something that felt both powerful and dangerous. The key was heavy in her hand, its surface etched with strange symbols that she couldn't quite decipher.

Daniel picked up one of the scrolls, carefully unrolling it to reveal a series of intricate drawings and strange, unfamiliar writing. "This stuff looks ancient," he said, his voice filled with wonder. "But why would anyone go to all this trouble for it?"

Clara's mind raced as she considered the possibilities. The objects in the chest were old, possibly valuable, but there was something more to them, something that went beyond simple monetary worth. The intruders had been willing to do whatever it took to get to this chest, to these objects, and that meant they were important—maybe even dangerous.

"We need to take this back upstairs," Clara said, her voice firm. "If this is what they're after, we can use it to our advantage."

Daniel nodded, carefully placing the scroll back in the chest. "Let's hurry. We don't know how much time we have."

They quickly gathered the objects from the chest, placing them into a small sack that Daniel had brought along. The key, the scrolls, the statues—everything that might be important or valuable. Clara couldn't shake the feeling that they were dealing with something far beyond their understanding, but they had no choice. They had to keep moving forward.

As they made their way back through the narrow passage-way, Clara's mind raced with questions. What were these objects? Why were the intruders so desperate to get their hands on them? And most importantly, how could they use them to survive?

When they finally emerged from the passageway and back into the basement, the cold, damp air was almost a relief. They had found something—something that might give them the upper hand. But as they made their way back up the stairs and into the main part of the inn, Clara couldn't shake the feeling that they were in even deeper danger than before.

They regrouped with Emma and Margaret in the lounge, their faces filled with a mixture of relief and apprehension as they saw the sack that Clara and Daniel had brought with them.

"What did you find?" Emma asked, her voice trembling with a mixture of fear and curiosity.

Clara set the sack down on the floor, carefully pulling out the objects they had found in the chest. The ornate key, the scrolls, the statues—they all seemed to carry a weight with them, a sense of history and mystery that was almost overwhelming.

"These," Clara said, her voice steady. "This is what they're after."

Margaret's eyes widened as she examined the objects, her expression a mixture of awe and fear. "But what are they? What do they do?"

"I don't know," Clara admitted. "But whatever they are, they're important. Important enough for those people to come after us, to try and scare us into giving them up."

Emma reached out to touch one of the scrolls, her fingers

trembling as they brushed against the ancient parchment. "Do you think… do you think they're cursed? Or… magical?"

The question hung in the air, heavy with implications. Clara didn't believe in curses or magic, but there was something about the objects that felt otherworldly, something that defied explanation. The symbols on the key, the strange writing on the scrolls—it all felt like pieces of a puzzle they couldn't quite solve.

"I don't know," Clara said finally, her voice filled with uncertainty. "But we need to be careful. We need to figure out what these are and how we can use them to survive."

Daniel nodded, his expression serious. "We should keep these hidden until we know more. If they come for us again, we'll be ready."

The group agreed, their fear tempered by a renewed sense of purpose. They had something the intruders wanted, something that could give them an advantage. But the danger was still very real, and they couldn't afford to let their guard down.

As they carefully hid the objects in a safe place, the fire in the hearth crackled softly, the flames casting long shadows on the walls. The wind howled outside, and the darkness pressed in on them from all sides, but they were still together, still fighting.

Clara knew that the night was far from over, and that the battle was only just beginning. But they had a weapon now, a tool that might help them turn the tables on their enemies. And as long as they had each other, there was hope.

The storm raged outside, and the shadows danced on the walls, but inside the inn, they were preparing for whatever came next. The game was far from over, and Clara was determined to see it through to the end.

17

Chapter 17

The morning light struggled to break through the thick clouds, casting a dull, gray pallor over the snow-covered landscape. Clara and Margaret bundled up in their heavy coats, bracing themselves against the biting cold as they stepped out of the inn. The previous night had been grueling, filled with tension and uncertainty, but now they had a new problem to solve: they were running low on firewood.

The remnants of the storm had left the ground thick with snow, making it difficult to move through the dense drifts. Clara's breath puffed out in small clouds as she trudged alongside Margaret, both of them carrying empty sacks to collect what firewood they could find. The trees surrounding the inn stood tall and silent, their branches heavy with snow, adding to the oppressive stillness that seemed to hang in the air.

As they moved farther away from the inn, Clara couldn't shake the feeling that something was wrong. The events of the past few days had left her on edge, and the eerie quiet of the morning did little to ease her nerves. Margaret seemed equally uneasy, her eyes constantly scanning their surroundings as they searched for firewood.

"Do you think Charles made it to town?" Margaret asked, her voice muffled by the scarf wrapped around her face.

Clara paused, considering the question. She wanted to believe that Charles had made it, that he would return with help, but the nagging doubt that had taken root in her mind was hard to ignore. "I hope so," she replied, trying to keep the worry out of her voice. "We need to stay focused. The more firewood we can gather, the better chance we have of staying warm until he gets back."

Margaret nodded, though her expression remained tense. "I just wish we knew what was going on. This whole thing… it doesn't make any sense."

Clara agreed, but she had no answers. The attack, the mysterious objects they had found in the basement, the relentless fear that seemed to stalk them at every turn—it was all part of a puzzle they couldn't yet solve. But they had to keep going, had to survive, if they ever hoped to understand what was happening.

They worked in silence, gathering as much wood as they could carry. The cold was relentless, seeping into their bones despite their heavy clothing. Clara's hands were numb, her fingers barely able to grip the rough wood as she piled it into her sack. But she pushed through the discomfort, focusing on the task at hand.

Just as they were finishing up, a piercing scream shattered the stillness of the morning. The sound echoed through the trees, cutting through the cold air like a knife.

Clara's heart leapt into her throat, her pulse quickening as she dropped the sack of firewood. "Margaret, did you hear that?"

Margaret's face went pale, her eyes wide with fear. "It came from the inn."

Without another word, they both took off running, the firewood forgotten as they raced back toward the inn. Clara's mind was racing, a thousand terrible possibilities flashing through her thoughts. The scream had been filled with terror, and the fear of what they might find when they returned gripped her like a vise.

The snow made it difficult to move quickly, but they pushed through, their breath coming in ragged gasps as they neared the inn. The building loomed ahead, its dark silhouette stark against the gray sky. Clara's heart pounded in her chest as they reached the door, her hand shaking as she pushed it open.

Inside, the scene that greeted them was chaos.

The living room was in disarray, furniture overturned, and the firewood they had gathered earlier scattered across the floor. Daniel lay unconscious on the ground, a deep gash on his forehead, blood trickling down his face. Emma was crouched in the corner, her eyes wide with terror, her hands covering her mouth as she watched the intruder—a man in a black balaclava—struggling to drag the sack of ancient objects they had hidden the night before.

Clara's blood ran cold as she took in the scene. The intruder had found their treasure, and he was trying to take it. But how had he known where to find it? How had he gotten inside without anyone noticing?

Before she could react, Margaret dashed across the room, her eyes locked on the intruder. "Stop!" she shouted, her voice filled with a mix of fear and determination.

The intruder didn't pause, didn't acknowledge Margaret's

presence as he continued to struggle with the heavy sack, his back turned to them. Clara's mind raced—if he got away with the treasure, they might lose their only leverage, their only chance of understanding what was happening.

But the intruder was too focused on his task to notice Margaret as she made a beeline for the kitchen. Clara watched in horror as Margaret flung open a drawer and pulled out the gun they had found in Alex's room and forgotten about until now.

"Margaret, wait—" Clara started, but it was too late.

Margaret aimed the gun at the intruder, her hands trembling as she struggled to keep the weapon steady. "I said stop!" she screamed, her voice shaking with a mix of fear and fury.

The intruder froze, finally turning to face her. Clara's breath caught in her throat as the man slowly raised his hands, his movements deliberate and measured. The room was deathly silent, the tension thick enough to cut with a knife.

"Margaret, put the gun down," Clara urged, her voice barely above a whisper. "We can handle this another way."

But Margaret didn't lower the gun. Her eyes were locked on the intruder, her hands still trembling. "Who are you?" she demanded, her voice wavering. "Why are you doing this?"

The intruder said nothing, his expression hidden behind the balaclava. His silence only seemed to fuel Margaret's anger, her desperation to understand what was happening.

Clara took a cautious step forward, her heart pounding in her chest. "Margaret, please—let's talk about this."

But before she could take another step, the intruder made a sudden move—reaching for something at his waist. In the blink of an eye, Margaret squeezed the trigger.

The gunshot rang out, deafening in the enclosed space. The

sound echoed off the walls, reverberating through the room like a thunderclap. The intruder staggered back, his body jerking with the impact of the bullet. For a moment, he seemed to hang in the air, suspended between life and death.

Then he crumpled to the floor, the sack of treasures spilling open beside him. The strange, ancient objects tumbled out, clattering to the ground with a sickening finality.

Clara's ears rang from the gunshot, her vision swimming as she struggled to make sense of what had just happened. Margaret stood frozen, the gun still clutched in her hands, her face pale and her eyes wide with shock.

For a long moment, no one moved. The room was eerily quiet, the only sound the faint crackling of the fire in the hearth. Clara's heart pounded in her chest as she forced herself to take a step forward, her breath coming in short, ragged gasps.

She reached the fallen intruder, her hands shaking as she knelt beside him. The balaclava covered his face, but there was no mistaking the familiar shape of his body, the lines of his jaw that she had come to know so well.

With trembling fingers, Clara pulled off the balaclava.

The sight that greeted her sent a jolt of shock through her entire body. It was Charles.

His eyes stared up at her, glassy and unseeing, his mouth slightly open as if he had been about to say something. The blood from the bullet wound pooled beneath him, staining the floor in a dark, spreading blot.

Clara's mind reeled, her thoughts a chaotic swirl of disbelief and horror. This couldn't be happening. Charles couldn't be… He had been their friend, their protector, the one who had gone out to find help. How could he be the one who had betrayed them?

Margaret let out a strangled sob, the gun slipping from her hands and clattering to the floor. She took a step back, her body trembling uncontrollably as she stared at Charles's lifeless form.

"Clara… I didn't… I didn't know…" Margaret's voice was choked with tears, her face a mask of horror and disbelief. "I didn't know it was him!"

Clara's own voice caught in her throat, her heart breaking as she looked down at Charles. The man she had trusted, the man they had all relied on, had been playing them from the start. He had been the enemy all along.

But why? The question hung in the air, unanswered, as Clara's mind struggled to comprehend what had just happened. Charles had gone out into the storm, claiming to seek help. But instead, he had returned to steal the treasure, to take what he had been after all along.

The realization hit her like a physical blow. Charles had never intended to bring back help. He had only been playing a part, gaining their trust so he could get close enough to take what he wanted. And now, because of that deception, he was dead.

Emma, who had been silently watching the scene unfold, finally found her voice. "He… he was one of them," she whispered, her eyes wide with shock. "He was with them all along…"

Clara nodded numbly, her mind still struggling to process the truth. "It looks that way," she said, her voice hollow. "He used us… all of us."

Margaret collapsed onto the floor, her hands clutching her face as sobs wracked her body. The realization that she had killed Charles—someone they had all trusted—was too much to bear. Clara moved to her side, wrapping her arms around Margaret in an attempt to comfort her, though she herself felt just as broken.

"It's not your fault," Clara whispered, though the words felt hollow even as she spoke them. "He deceived us all. We had no way of knowing."

Margaret shook her head, her tears soaking into Clara's coat. "But I... I pulled the trigger. I killed him. I—" Her voice broke into a sob, and she buried her face in Clara's shoulder.

Emma remained rooted in place, her eyes fixated on Charles's body. The shock was evident in her expression, but there was also a dawning realization, a connection forming in her mind as she tried to piece together the events that had led to this moment.

Daniel groaned from the floor, regaining consciousness as the world slowly came back into focus. Clara gently released Margaret and hurried over to him, helping him sit up. His face was pale, and he winced as he touched the gash on his forehead.

"What... what happened?" Daniel asked, his voice weak, confusion clouding his eyes.

Clara hesitated, unsure of how to explain the betrayal, the violence that had just unfolded. But there was no way to soften the truth. "It was Charles," she said quietly. "He... he was the one who attacked you. Margaret... she shot him."

Daniel's eyes widened in shock, his gaze snapping to the lifeless body on the floor. "Charles? But... why? Why would he do this?"

Clara shook her head, her voice trembling as she replied, "I don't know. But it's clear now—he was working with the others all along. This was all part of their plan."

The room fell into a heavy silence as they all tried to process the magnitude of what had just happened. The man they had trusted, the man they had relied on to protect them, had been their enemy from the start. The betrayal cut deep, leaving them all reeling with a sense of disbelief and anger.

Emma finally broke the silence, her voice trembling as she spoke. "What do we do now? If Charles was working with them, then… there must be more of them out there, right? They're not going to stop."

Clara's mind raced as she considered their options. They had lost one of their own, but they had also gained crucial information—Charles had been after the treasure, the ancient objects they had found in the hidden chamber. Whatever these objects were, they were important enough for him to betray them, to risk everything to get his hands on them.

"We need to secure the inn," Clara said, her voice steadier now as she forced herself to focus. "There could be more of them coming. We can't let our guard down."

Daniel, still reeling from the betrayal, nodded in agreement. "We should barricade the doors and windows again. We need to make sure no one else can get in."

Margaret, still shaken, wiped away her tears and tried to compose herself. "I'll help," she said, though her voice was unsteady. "We can't let them take the treasure. We can't let Charles's death be for nothing."

Clara squeezed Margaret's shoulder, offering her a small, reassuring nod. "We'll make sure his sacrifice wasn't in vain. But first, we need to protect ourselves."

The group moved quickly, setting about securing the inn as best they could. The barricades were reinforced, furniture was piled against doors and windows, and anything that could be used as a weapon was gathered and distributed. The fear of another attack hung heavy over them, but they were determined not to be caught off guard again.

As they worked, Clara's mind kept returning to the treasure—the strange, ancient objects that had caused so much death and destruction. There was something more to them, something they didn't yet understand. Charles had been willing to kill for them, and that meant they were powerful, possibly dangerous.

Once the inn was as secure as they could make it, Clara gathered the group in the lounge, the fire crackling softly in the hearth as they sat around the scattered treasure. The room felt different now, the air heavy with the weight of their losses and the knowledge that they were up against something far more sinister than they had realized.

"We need to figure out what these objects are," Clara said, her voice calm but filled with urgency. "If we understand what we're dealing with, we might be able to use them to our advantage."

Emma looked uncertain, her gaze drifting to the ancient scrolls and the strange, intricately carved statues. "But how? We don't even know where they came from, or what they're supposed to do."

Clara picked up the large, ornate key, its cold metal surface etched with symbols that seemed to pulse with a life of their own. "We start with what we do know. Charles wanted these objects—he was willing to betray us, to risk his life to get them. That means they're valuable, maybe even powerful."

Daniel, his face still pale from the head wound, leaned forward, his eyes narrowing as he examined the objects more closely. "These symbols… they don't look like anything I've ever seen before. They're not just decorations. They mean something."

Margaret, still shaken but determined, spoke up. "I don't think we should try to use them until we understand what they are. They could be dangerous."

Clara nodded in agreement. "We need to be careful, but we also need to be proactive. If Charles was after these, then whoever he was working with will come looking for them. We can't just sit and wait for them to find us."

Emma hesitated, then asked the question that had been on all their minds. "Do you think… do you think we should leave the inn? Try to get away before they come back?"

The idea of leaving the relative safety of the inn, venturing out into the unknown, was terrifying. But staying put might be just as dangerous. Clara weighed the options, her mind racing with the possible outcomes. If they stayed, they could fortify the inn and try to fend off any further attacks. But if they left, they would be vulnerable, exposed to the elements and to whoever was out there hunting them.

"I don't know if leaving is the right answer," Clara admitted. "But if we stay, we need to be prepared. We can't rely on anyone coming to save us—not after what happened with Charles. We have to assume we're on our own."

Daniel nodded, his expression grim. "Then we need a plan. If they come for us again, we need to be ready to fight back."

Clara agreed, though the thought of more violence, more bloodshed, filled her with dread. But they had no choice. They were trapped in a deadly game, and the only way to survive was to fight.

"We'll take turns keeping watch," Clara said, taking charge. "We can't let them catch us off guard again. And we'll need to start rationing our supplies—we don't know how long we'll be stuck here."

Margaret and Emma nodded in agreement, though the fear in their eyes was evident. The reality of their situation was beginning to sink in, and it was clear that they all understood the gravity of what they were up against.

The day passed slowly, each hour dragging on with agonizing tension. The group took turns keeping watch, their eyes constantly scanning the windows and doors for any sign of movement. The fear of another attack, of another betrayal, was ever-present, gnawing at their nerves.

Clara couldn't stop thinking about Charles—about how they had trusted him, relied on him, only to be betrayed in the worst possible way. The image of his lifeless body, his eyes staring up at her in death, haunted her every thought. But she couldn't afford to dwell on it. They were still in danger, and they had to stay focused.

As the day began to fade into evening, Clara gathered the group once more in the lounge. The fire was burning low, casting long shadows across the room as they huddled together, the ancient objects laid out before them.

"We need to make a decision," Clara said, her voice steady but filled with urgency. "Do we stay and try to defend the inn, or do we take our chances and try to leave?"

The question hung in the air, heavy with the weight of their situation. There was no easy answer, no right choice. But they had to decide, and they had to do it soon.

Margaret spoke first, her voice filled with resolve. "I think we should stay. This inn is the only shelter we have. If we leave, we'll be exposed to the cold, the snow… and to them. Here, at least we have walls around us."

Emma nodded in agreement. "And we have the fire, the food we've stored. If we leave, we might not survive out there."

Daniel, though clearly conflicted, finally agreed. "Staying might be our best option. But we need to be ready. If they come for us, we can't hesitate. We have to fight."

Clara looked around at her friends, at the fear and determination etched into their faces, and knew they were right. Leaving the inn would be too dangerous, too risky. They had to stay, and they had to be ready to defend themselves.

"Alright," Clara said, her voice filled with a steely resolve. "We stay. We fortify the inn, we protect the treasure, and we make sure that if they come for us again, they don't get what they want."

The group nodded in agreement, their fear tempered by a renewed sense of purpose. They had made their decision, and now they had to stand by it.

As the evening deepened into night, the wind outside picked up, howling through the trees and rattling the windows. The fire crackled in the hearth, its warmth a small comfort against the cold and darkness that surrounded them.

Clara took the first watch, her eyes fixed on the windows as the others tried to rest. The fear of what might come next gnawed at her, but she refused to let it control her. They had made it this far, and they would make it through the night.

But as the shadows danced on the walls and the wind howled outside, Clara couldn't shake the feeling that the worst was yet to come. The game was far from over, and the enemy was still out there, waiting for the right moment to strike.

But this time, they would be ready.

18

Chapter 18

The gray morning light filtered through the thick curtains of the inn, casting a dim glow over the room. Outside, the storm had calmed, leaving behind a blanket of snow that seemed to mute the world beyond the windows. But inside the inn, the atmosphere was anything but calm.

Clara sat at the small kitchen table, her hands wrapped around a mug of lukewarm tea. She had barely slept, her mind too full of conflicting thoughts to allow for any real rest. The events of the past few days had left her emotionally drained, but she knew that today would bring more challenges, more difficult decisions.

As she stared into the swirling tea, the sound of hushed voices reached her from the next room. The tension in those voices was unmistakable, and it set Clara on edge. She had sensed the growing unease among the group, the fractures that were beginning to form under the pressure of their situation. And now, it seemed, those fractures were about to deepen.

Clara rose from the table, leaving the half-finished tea behind as she made her way into the living room. The sight that greeted her confirmed her fears—Sarah, Emma, and Daniel were standing near the hearth, their expressions tense and angry as they argued with Margaret. The three men they had taken captive—Charles's accomplices—were still bound and huddled together in a corner, their eyes downcast as they listened to the rising voices.

"Margaret, you can't be serious!" Sarah's voice was sharp, edged with frustration. "We're running low on food as it is, and you're wasting our rations on them? They're the reason we're in this mess!"

Margaret's face was pale but resolute as she stood her ground. "They're human beings, Sarah. We can't just let them starve."

"They wouldn't hesitate to do the same to us," Emma interjected, her voice colder than Clara had ever heard it. "They tried to kill us. Why should we care what happens to them?"

Daniel nodded in agreement, his arms crossed over his chest. "We can't afford to be soft right now, Margaret. We're barely holding it together as it is. We have to think about our survival."

Clara felt a pang of anxiety as she listened to the argument unfold. The divide between the group was growing wider, and she could see how deeply this issue was affecting them. Margaret was standing alone, facing down three of their friends who were united in their anger and fear. Clara knew she had to say something, but she wasn't sure what.

"Maybe we should think this through," Clara said cautiously, stepping into the room. "We need to consider all the options."

Sarah turned to Clara, her frustration evident in the tightness of her jaw. "What's there to consider? We don't have enough food to go around, and we can't keep feeding the people who've been trying to kill us."

Margaret's eyes filled with a mixture of desperation and defiance as she looked to Clara for support. "Clara, we can't just let them die. What does that make us if we do?"

Clara felt the weight of their expectations pressing down on her, the responsibility of making a decision that could have serious consequences for all of them. She understood Sarah, Emma, and Daniel's concerns—every scrap of food was vital to their survival. But at the same time, she couldn't ignore Margaret's plea. What kind of people would they become if they started letting others starve, even if those others had been their enemies?

"We need to consider what's at stake here," Clara said, her voice steady despite the turmoil inside her. "We're in a dangerous situation, and we're all under a lot of stress. But we have to be careful not to lose sight of who we are."

Emma let out a bitter laugh, shaking her head. "Who we are? Clara, we're fighting for our lives. This isn't about being nice or doing the right thing—it's about surviving."

Margaret's voice trembled as she responded, "But what if surviving means becoming just like them? What if it means losing our humanity?"

The room fell into a tense silence as the group grappled with the implications of Margaret's words. Clara could see the conflict in their eyes, the way they were torn between self-preservation and the desire to hold on to some semblance of morality in the face of unimaginable fear.

Daniel finally broke the silence, his voice low and filled with frustration. "If we keep feeding them, we're going to run out of food a lot faster. We'll be putting ourselves at risk for nothing. They're not going to help us. They're not going to change their ways just because we've shown them kindness."

Margaret's resolve seemed to waver, but she didn't back down. "I know it's risky, but I can't just let them starve. I won't."

Sarah's eyes flashed with anger as she stepped closer to Margaret. "And what about us, Margaret? What happens when we run out of food? Are you going to let us starve too? Is that the kind of decision you want to make?"

Clara could see the growing desperation in Sarah's expression, the fear that was driving her anger. It wasn't just about the food—it was about the constant pressure they were all under, the fear that every decision they made could be the difference between life and death.

Margaret looked away, her shoulders slumping as she struggled with the weight of the argument. "I don't know what the right answer is," she admitted, her voice small. "But I can't be the one to decide who lives and who dies."

The room was thick with tension, the divide between the group now more apparent than ever. Clara felt torn, her own emotions pulling her in different directions. On one hand, she understood the need to be practical, to conserve their resources and protect themselves. But on the other hand, she couldn't shake the feeling that they would be crossing a line if they let these men starve.

"I think we need to take a step back," Clara said finally, trying to diffuse the situation. "We're all exhausted, and this decision is too important to make when we're this upset. Let's take some time to think it over, and then we can decide together what to do."

Emma shook her head, her frustration evident. "Clara, we don't have time to wait. Every minute we spend feeding them is a minute closer to us running out of food."

Daniel nodded in agreement, his expression hardening. "We need to be decisive. If we don't make the hard choices now, we might not get another chance."

Clara felt the pressure mounting, the weight of the decision pressing down on her from all sides. She knew that whatever choice they made, it would have consequences—both for their survival and for the way they saw themselves, and each other.

"We can't let this tear us apart," Clara said, her voice filled with a quiet intensity. "We need to stay united if we're going to get through this."

Sarah's voice was sharp as she replied, "Then maybe we need to start making decisions that keep us united, Clara. We can't afford to be soft."

The words stung, but Clara knew that Sarah's frustration was coming from a place of fear. They were all scared, all struggling to cope with the unimaginable stress of their situation. But that didn't make the decision any easier.

Margaret's voice broke through the tension, soft but firm. "I'll take responsibility for them," she said quietly. "If we decide to feed them, I'll give up my own rations. I can't let them die, but I also don't want to put anyone else at risk."

The room fell into a heavy silence as the group considered Margaret's offer. It was a compromise, but it wasn't a perfect solution. The divide between them was still there, the fractures that had formed threatening to deepen further.

Emma looked at Margaret, her expression a mix of frustration and pity. "You're not thinking clearly, Margaret. You're letting your emotions cloud your judgment."

Margaret shook her head, her eyes filled with a quiet determination. "Maybe I am. But I can't help it. I won't let them die if there's something I can do to stop it."

Clara watched the exchange, her heart heavy with the knowledge that this argument was only the beginning. The tension between them wasn't going away, and the decisions they made in the coming days would either bring them closer together or drive them further apart.

Sarah sighed, her anger giving way to exhaustion. "Fine. If you want to give up your own rations, that's your choice. But don't expect us to go along with it if it starts affecting our chances of survival."

Emma nodded in agreement, her expression softening slightly. "We'll see how it goes. But if things start to get worse, we need to be prepared to make the hard choices."

Daniel remained silent, his face unreadable as he stared into the fire. Clara could see the conflict in his eyes, the way he was struggling to reconcile the need for survival with the moral implications of their decisions.

Clara took a deep breath, trying to steady herself as she spoke. "We'll take it one day at a time. If it becomes clear that we can't sustain feeding them, we'll have to reassess. But for now, we need to stay focused on keeping ourselves safe."

The group nodded in agreement, though the tension between them was still palpable. The argument had revealed the cracks in their unity, and Clara knew that it would take more than a few words to mend those cracks.

As the day wore on, the inn felt different—heavier, more oppressive. The fear of what lay ahead hung over them like a dark cloud, and the divide between them seemed to grow wider with each passing hour. Clara could feel the strain in every interaction, the way their words were tinged with unspoken doubts and fears.

Margaret spent much of the day tending to the captives, bringing them small portions of food and water, her face drawn with worry. The men remained silent, their expressions blank as they accepted the meager offerings. They were prisoners, but they were also the source of the group's growing unease.

Clara found herself drifting between tasks, her mind racing with thoughts of what had happened and what was still to come. The argument had shaken her more than she wanted to admit, and she couldn't shake the feeling that they were on the brink of something dangerous—something that could tear them apart for good.

As the sun began to set, casting long shadows across the snow-covered landscape, Clara stood by the window, staring out at the endless white expanse. The world outside seemed so vast, so unforgiving, and she couldn't help but feel small and powerless in the face of it all.

Sarah joined her at the window, her expression softening as she looked out at the same bleak scene. "I'm sorry, Clara," she said quietly. "I know this isn't easy for any of us. I just… I'm scared. I'm scared that we're not going to make it."

Clara nodded, her voice barely above a whisper. "I'm scared too. But we have to try. We have to hold on to whatever hope we have left."

Sarah's eyes filled with tears, and she reached out to squeeze Clara's hand. "We'll get through this. We have to."

Clara squeezed Sarah's hand in return, drawing strength from the small gesture. They were still a team, still fighting for survival. But the fractures that had formed were real, and Clara knew that it would take everything they had to hold on to each other in the days to come.

As the darkness of night settled over the inn, Clara felt the weight of the decision they had made pressing down on her. The tension between them was still there, simmering just beneath the surface, and she knew that it wouldn't take much to push them over the edge.

But for now, they were still together. They were still fighting.

And as long as they had each other, there was still hope.

19

Chapter 19

The night pressed in around the inn, thick with the kind of darkness that seemed to swallow sound and light alike. The fire in the hearth had burned down to embers, casting faint, flickering shadows on the walls. Clara sat in the dimly lit room, her mind racing as she stared at the three men who were bound and gagged in the corner. The fear that had been gnawing at her all day was still there, but now it was accompanied by a grim determination. She knew they needed answers, and these men—Charles's accomplices—were the only ones who could provide them.

Margaret had fallen into an uneasy sleep on the sofa, her breathing shallow and restless. Emma and Daniel were sitting near the fire, their expressions tense as they watched Clara pace the room. Sarah was perched on the edge of a chair, her gaze fixed on the captives with a mix of suspicion and fear.

Clara stopped pacing and turned to face the group. "We need to make a decision," she said quietly, her voice cutting through the stillness of the room. "We can't keep going on like this—not knowing who these men are or what they want. We need answers."

Sarah nodded, her jaw clenched with tension. "But they won't talk. We've tried questioning them, and they've said nothing."

Clara looked at the captives, their eyes dark and unreadable behind the gags. She knew Sarah was right—the men had remained silent, even as their situation grew more desperate. But Clara wasn't willing to give up just yet.

"What if we make them an offer?" Clara suggested, her voice steady despite the uncertainty she felt. "If they talk—if they tell us who they are, who they're working for—then we'll give them rations. It's their decision. If they want to eat, they'll have to talk."

Emma frowned, her brow furrowed in thought. "Do you really think that will work? They've been silent this whole time. What makes you think they'll start talking now?"

Clara shrugged, though the gesture felt heavier than it should have. "It's worth a try. And this way, the decision is theirs, not ours. We won't be deciding whether they live or die—they will."

Daniel leaned forward, his expression serious. "It's a gamble, but it might be our best shot at getting some answers. If they want to survive, they'll have to cooperate."

Margaret stirred on the sofa, her eyes fluttering open as she listened to the conversation. "But what if they still won't talk? What do we do then?"

Clara's heart sank at the thought, but she pushed it aside. "Then we're no worse off than we are now. But at least we'll know we tried."

The group exchanged tense glances, each of them weighing the risks and potential rewards of Clara's plan. The tension between them was still there, simmering just below the surface, but Clara could see that they all understood the necessity of the situation. They couldn't afford to remain in the dark any longer.

Sarah was the first to speak, her voice filled with a mix of resignation and resolve. "Alright. Let's try it. But if they won't talk… then we need to figure out what we're going to do with them."

Clara nodded, her expression grim. "Agreed."

With the plan settled, Clara approached the captives, her heart pounding in her chest. She could feel the weight of the others' eyes on her as she knelt down in front of the men, her voice low and steady as she spoke.

"We're giving you a choice," she said, her gaze flicking between their faces. "If you start talking—if you tell us who you are and why you're here—we'll give you food and water. But if you stay silent… then you'll have to live with the consequences."

The men stared at her, their expressions blank, their eyes betraying nothing. Clara felt a cold knot of anxiety tighten in her stomach as she waited for a response, but none came. The silence stretched on, thick and oppressive, until Clara finally stepped back, her heart sinking.

"They're not going to talk," Emma said, her voice heavy with frustration.

"Give them time," Clara replied, though her own hope was waning. "They might change their minds once they realize what's at stake."

The group agreed to give the men a few hours to consider their options, though the tension in the room was palpable. As the night wore on, they kept a close watch on the captives, but the men remained stubbornly silent, their expressions cold and defiant.

Clara tried to sleep, but her mind refused to stay quiet. She lay awake, listening to the wind howl outside, her thoughts a chaotic swirl of fear and doubt. What if the men never talked? What if they never got the answers they so desperately needed?

Eventually, exhaustion took over, and Clara drifted into a fitful sleep, haunted by nightmares of shadowy figures and unanswered questions.

The next morning, Clara awoke with a start, her heart pounding in her chest. The room was still dim, the early morning light barely breaking through the heavy curtains. She sat up, her mind groggy with sleep, and immediately sensed that something was wrong.

The others were already awake, their faces pale and filled with shock as they stood near the corner where the captives had been kept. Clara's stomach churned with dread as she got to her feet, her legs unsteady beneath her.

"What's going on?" she asked, her voice thick with sleep and fear.

Emma turned to her, her eyes wide with horror. "Clara… they're dead."

Clara's breath caught in her throat as she pushed past the others, her heart racing as she reached the corner where the captives had been held. The sight that greeted her was like something out of a nightmare.

All three men lay on the floor, their throats slashed open, blood pooling around their bodies in dark, sticky puddles. Their eyes were open, staring sightlessly at the ceiling, their expressions frozen in the final moments of their lives.

Clara's mind went blank, the shock of what she was seeing

overwhelming her senses. For a moment, she couldn't move, couldn't think—only stand there, staring at the gruesome scene before her.

"How... how did this happen?" Sarah's voice was trembling, her face as white as a sheet.

Daniel shook his head, his own shock evident in the way his hands trembled as he ran them through his hair. "I don't know... I don't know how this could have happened without us hearing anything."

Margaret was shaking, her hands pressed to her mouth as she stared at the dead men, tears streaming down her face. "Who... who could have done this?"

Clara finally forced herself to move, her body feeling heavy and sluggish as she knelt beside the bodies. The cuts were clean, precise—whoever had done this had known exactly what they were doing.

"They were murdered," Clara said quietly, her voice hollow. "Someone killed them while we were sleeping."

The room fell into a stunned silence as the group absorbed the gravity of what had just happened. The realization that there was a killer among them—a killer who had struck without warning, without remorse—sent a wave of fear and paranoia rippling through the group.

Sarah was the first to voice what they were all thinking. "Who did this? One of us... one of us must have done this."

Emma shook her head, her face contorted with disbelief. "No... no, that can't be. We're all in this together. We would never... we wouldn't..."

"But look at them!" Daniel's voice was sharp, filled with a mix of fear and anger. "Someone did this. Someone among us."

Margaret's tears had turned to quiet sobs as she stared at the bodies, her voice trembling as she spoke. "But why? Why would anyone do this?"

Clara's mind raced as she tried to make sense of the situation. The idea that one of them could have killed the men was horrifying, but there was no other explanation. The men had been tied up, helpless—there was no way they could have killed each other.

"Whoever did this didn't want them to talk," Clara said, her voice quiet but filled with a grim certainty. "They were silenced before they could give us any answers."

Sarah's eyes narrowed as she looked around the room, her suspicion clear. "So who didn't want them to talk? Who had the most to lose if they did?"

The question hung in the air, heavy with implications. Clara felt a cold knot of fear tighten in her stomach as she looked at her friends, the people she had trusted with her life. Could one of them really have done this? Could one of them be hiding something so terrible that they were willing to kill to keep it secret?

Daniel's face was pale, his expression filled with anger and fear. "We need to figure out who did this, and we need to do it now. We can't stay here with a killer among us."

Emma looked around at the group, her eyes filled with desperation. "But how? How do we find out who did this?"

Clara took a deep breath, trying to steady herself as she spoke. "We need to stay calm. We need to think this through. Whoever did this… they must have had a reason. We need to figure out what that reason is."

Margaret wiped her tears, her voice barely above a whisper. "But what if… what if we never find out? What if we're stuck here, never knowing who we can trust?"

Clara's heart ached at the thought, but she knew that they couldn't afford to let fear and paranoia consume them. They were already teetering on the edge, and one wrong move could push them over into complete chaos.

Clara forced herself to stand, her legs trembling slightly as she looked around at the others. "We have to stick together," she said, her voice steady despite the turmoil inside her. "If we start turning on each other, then whoever did this wins. We need to figure out what happened, but we can't do that if we're at each other's throats."

Sarah crossed her arms, her expression hardening. "So what do you suggest, Clara? How do we figure out who did this without accusing each other?"

Clara looked at the bodies on the floor, the gruesome evidence of betrayal that had shattered what little trust remained among them. She knew that they had to tread carefully, that one wrong word could ignite the tension simmering beneath the surface.

"We need to start by asking ourselves who had the opportunity to do this," Clara said slowly, her mind racing. "We all went to bed around the same time, but someone must have stayed awake or woken up in the middle of the night. Did anyone hear anything? See anything unusual?"

The room fell into a tense silence as each person considered the question. Margaret shook her head, still visibly shaken. "I didn't hear anything… I was so exhausted, I fell asleep almost as soon as I lay down."

Emma nodded in agreement. "Same here. I didn't wake up at all until this morning."

Sarah's brow furrowed in thought. "I was up for a little while, just thinking… but I didn't hear or see anything. It was too quiet, honestly."

Daniel, who had been staring at the bodies with a look of deep unease, finally spoke up. "I was on watch for a couple of hours. I didn't hear anything, either… but I did doze off toward the end. I'm sorry. I should have stayed awake."

Clara sighed, frustration gnawing at her. They were getting nowhere. Whoever had done this had been careful, deliberate. There were no signs, no clues—just the cold, brutal fact that three men were dead, and one of them had to be responsible.

"Okay," Clara said, trying to remain calm. "If no one heard or saw anything, then we need to consider motives. Why would someone want to kill these men?"

Sarah's voice was sharp as she replied, "The obvious answer is that someone didn't want them to talk. Someone was afraid of what they might say."

Emma's eyes widened, and she looked around at the group, fear creeping into her voice. "But that would mean… one of us is hiding something. Something worth killing for."

The room grew colder as the implication settled over them. The idea that one of their own could be capable of such violence, such betrayal, was almost too much to bear. But they couldn't ignore the truth, no matter how much they wanted to.

"Who would have the most to lose if the men talked?" Daniel asked, his gaze shifting between the others. "Did anyone seem particularly nervous about the idea of questioning them?"

Clara's mind raced as she considered the question. Had anyone seemed especially on edge? Had anyone been more insistent than the others about keeping the men alive—or about not questioning them too harshly?

Margaret, her voice still trembling, spoke up. "I... I was the one who didn't want them to die. But I swear, I didn't do this. I wouldn't... I couldn't..."

Clara's heart ached for Margaret, but she knew they couldn't afford to let emotions cloud their judgment. "Margaret, we're not accusing you. But we need to consider every possibility. Did anyone else seem particularly invested in keeping them alive—or in silencing them?"

Emma shook her head, looking helpless. "I don't know. We were all scared, all trying to figure out what to do. I didn't notice anything out of the ordinary."

Sarah's gaze shifted to Daniel, suspicion flickering in her eyes. "You were on watch, Daniel. You had the opportunity."

Daniel's expression darkened, anger flaring in his eyes. "Are you accusing me, Sarah? I was doing my job, trying to keep us safe. I fell asleep, yes, but I didn't kill anyone."

Sarah's voice was cold as she replied, "I'm just saying, you were the last one awake. If someone did this after the rest of us were asleep, it could have been you."

Clara quickly stepped between them, holding up her hands to stop the argument before it escalated further. "We're not going to start pointing fingers without evidence. We need to stay calm, stay rational. If we start accusing each other without proof, we're going to tear ourselves apart."

Daniel's anger simmered, but he didn't press the issue. He turned away, frustration etched into his features. Sarah, too, backed down, though Clara could see the suspicion still lingering in her eyes.

"We need to keep an eye on each other," Clara said, her voice firm. "No one goes anywhere alone. We need to stay together, stay vigilant. Whoever did this might try something again."

Margaret looked around the room, fear and sadness etched into her face. "But what if we never find out who did it? What if we're stuck here, always wondering who we can trust?"

Clara didn't have an answer. The fear of the unknown, the creeping paranoia that was beginning to infect them all, was the most dangerous enemy they faced. But she knew they couldn't give in to it. They had to keep going, had to stay united—even if that unity was now fractured and fragile.

"We'll figure it out," Clara said, though the words felt hollow. "But for now, we need to focus on survival. We can't afford to let this divide us any more than it already has."

The group nodded, though Clara could see the doubt and fear in their eyes. The atmosphere in the inn had shifted dramatically, from one of desperate cooperation to one of wary suspicion. Trust had been shattered, and it would take more than words to rebuild it.

As the day wore on, the group moved through their tasks in silence, the weight of the morning's discovery hanging over them like a dark cloud. The bodies of the three men were carefully wrapped in sheets and moved to a cold, unused room in the inn, a makeshift morgue that added to the growing sense of dread that permeated the building.

Clara tried to focus on the practical tasks at hand—gathering more firewood, rationing their dwindling supplies, reinforcing the barricades—but her mind kept returning to the question that haunted them all: Who had killed the men, and why?

As evening approached, the group gathered in the lounge, their faces drawn and exhausted. The tension between them was palpable, and Clara could feel the unspoken accusations simmering beneath the surface.

"We need to make a plan for tonight," Daniel said, his voice tight with strain. "We can't afford to let our guard down again."

Sarah nodded, her expression grim. "We'll take shifts, two people at a time. No one is awake alone."

Emma, who had been quiet for most of the day, spoke up. "But what if… what if the person who did this is on watch with someone else? How do we know we can trust them?"

The question sent a shiver through the group, the reality of their situation becoming increasingly clear. They were trapped in the inn, surrounded by snow and darkness, with no way of knowing who among them was a murderer.

Clara took a deep breath, trying to steady herself as she addressed the group. "We don't have any other choice. We have to trust each other, at least enough to get through this. If we let fear control us, then we're already lost."

The group agreed, though the unease in the room was palpable. The night ahead would be long, filled with uncertainty and fear, but they had no other option. They had to keep watch, had to stay vigilant—and hope that the killer wouldn't strike again.

As they settled into their shifts, the inn was plunged into darkness, the only light coming from the flickering fire in the hearth. The wind howled outside, and the silence inside the inn was thick and oppressive, broken only by the occasional creak of the old wooden beams.

Clara sat by the fire, her eyes heavy with exhaustion as she kept watch with Daniel. The tension between them was thick, the memory of Sarah's accusation still fresh in their minds. But they didn't speak of it, choosing instead to sit in uneasy silence, listening to the wind and the crackle of the fire.

As the night wore on, Clara's thoughts drifted to the men who had been killed, the silence that had haunted them even in death. Whoever had murdered them had known exactly what they were doing—had known how to kill swiftly and silently. And that thought filled Clara with a deep, unsettling fear.

The night passed slowly, each minute stretching into an eternity as Clara and Daniel kept their vigil. But as the first light of dawn began to filter through the windows, a sense of relief washed over them. They had made it through the night without incident, but the tension between them remained, unspoken but ever-present.

As the others woke and gathered in the lounge, Clara couldn't shake the feeling that they were all standing on the edge of a precipice, one wrong move away from disaster. The bonds that had once held them together were fraying, and she knew that it would take everything they had to keep from falling apart.

20

Chapter 20

The morning light filtered softly through the curtains, casting a pale glow across the inn's weathered floors. For the first time in what felt like days, the night had passed without incident, the stillness of the early hours offering a brief reprieve from the tension that had consumed them. But even as the sun crept higher in the sky, Clara couldn't shake the feeling of unease that lingered like a shadow.

She had kept watch through the last hours of the night, her eyes heavy with exhaustion, but her mind too restless to allow for sleep. Now, with the others slowly stirring from their uneasy slumber, Clara felt the weight of the past few days pressing down on her, a constant, suffocating presence that left her feeling trapped and isolated.

Needing a moment to herself, Clara decided to retreat to her room. The thought of lighting the fire and sitting in quiet solitude was an appealing one—she needed space to think, to process everything that had happened and try to make sense of the tangled web of lies and betrayals that had ensnared them all.

Clara slipped away from the lounge unnoticed, the others too preoccupied with their own thoughts to pay her any mind. As she made her way down the narrow hallway to her room, the floorboards creaked beneath her feet, the sound a reminder of how old and fragile the inn truly was.

Once inside her room, Clara closed the door behind her and leaned against it for a moment, letting out a long, slow breath. The air was cold, and she shivered as she crossed the room to the fireplace. With practiced movements, she knelt and began stacking logs, kindling, and old newspaper in the hearth. She struck a match and held it to the kindling, watching as the flames slowly took hold, growing from a small flicker to a warm, crackling fire.

As the room filled with the comforting warmth of the fire, Clara sank into the worn armchair by the window, her gaze drifting to the snow-covered landscape outside. The world beyond the inn was still and peaceful, a stark contrast to the turmoil that had been brewing inside. But the peace outside was deceptive, and Clara knew it couldn't last.

Alone with her thoughts, Clara began to replay the events of the past few days, her mind sifting through the details, searching for answers in the chaos. She thought of Emma—how she had always seemed on edge, her nerves frayed from the moment she arrived. Emma had been one of the first to voice her distrust of the others, especially of Charles. But now Clara couldn't help but wonder if Emma's anxiety had been about more than just fear of their situation.

Charles's betrayal was another piece of the puzzle that Clara couldn't ignore. She had trusted him—trusted him to lead, to protect them, to be a friend. But Charles had been playing them from the start, working with the very people who had turned their lives into a nightmare. The realization still stung, and Clara couldn't shake the anger and hurt that came with it. How had she been so blind?

Clara's thoughts turned to Daniel and Sarah. She had been suspicious of them when she first arrived at the inn, their connection to Alex—an enigma in his own right—too coincidental to ignore. Alex had been the catalyst, stirring up trouble and sowing seeds of doubt among them all. And those names on his list, the ones that had been crossed off—Clara had never found out what they meant, but she had a feeling they were more important than any of them realized.

She tried to piece together everything she knew, but the more she thought about it, the more tangled the threads became. Why had Sarah and Daniel been in Alex's room that night? What had they been looking for, and why had they never spoken of it afterward? Clara's suspicion deepened as she considered the possibility that there was more to their story than they had let on.

And then there was Margaret. Sweet, kind Margaret, who had been so devastated by Charles's betrayal. But how could she not have suspected anything? Charles had been coming to the inn for years—surely she must have noticed something off about him, something that didn't add up. Or had she simply turned a blind eye, unwilling to see the truth about the man she considered a friend?

Clara's mind raced as she tried to connect the dots, the pieces of the puzzle refusing to fit together in any coherent way. But one thing was becoming increasingly clear: she couldn't trust anyone. Not fully, not anymore. They had all kept secrets, all played their part in the web of lies that had ensnared them. And if she wanted to survive, if she wanted to find out the truth, she would have to rely on herself.

A cold, hard resolve settled over Clara as she came to this realization. From now on, she was on her own. She would have to navigate the dangerous currents of suspicion and deceit without letting anyone know how much she had pieced together. It was a dangerous game, but one she was determined to win.

As the fire crackled and popped in the hearth, Clara let her mind drift back to the moments that had led them to this point. She thought of the first night they had all gathered in the lounge, still strangers to one another but united by the circumstances that had brought them together. How quickly that unity had unraveled, frayed by fear and mistrust.

She thought of Alex—how he had arrived at the inn like a storm, upending everything in his path. He had been the one to plant the seeds of doubt, to fan the flames of suspicion. And yet, even now, Clara couldn't quite bring herself to hate him. He had been enigmatic, yes, but there had been something more to him, something she still couldn't fully grasp.

And those names on his list—why had some been crossed off? What did it mean? Had Alex known something about the danger they were all in, something that had made him act the way he did? Clara couldn't shake the feeling that the answer to that question was crucial, but without more information, it was just another piece of the puzzle that didn't fit.

She thought of Emma again, how nervous she had seemed from the start. Had it been simply fear, or was there something deeper at play? Was Emma hiding something, or had she simply been a victim of the same paranoia that had gripped them all?

And what about Sarah and Daniel? Their presence at the

inn had never quite made sense to Clara, and the more she thought about it, the more convinced she became that they were hiding something. Why had they been in Alex's room? What had they been looking for? Clara knew she would have to keep a close eye on them, to watch for any clues that might reveal their true intentions.

Margaret's involvement—or lack thereof—was another mystery that gnawed at Clara. How could she not have seen through Charles's facade? Was it willful ignorance, or something more sinister? Clara couldn't shake the feeling that Margaret's kindness, her insistence on feeding the captives, was part of a larger pattern, something she hadn't yet fully understood.

As the fire burned low, Clara's thoughts continued to swirl, each new realization adding another layer of complexity to the tangled web she was trying to unravel. She was more certain than ever that she couldn't trust anyone, but she also knew that she couldn't let them see her suspicion. She would have to play along, pretend to go along with the group, while quietly gathering the information she needed to uncover the truth.

Clara rose from the armchair, the weight of her thoughts heavy on her shoulders as she made her way back down the hallway to the lounge. She would observe the others, watch their interactions, and listen carefully to everything they said. If there were answers to be found, she would find them—but she would have to be careful, patient. One wrong move, and the fragile truce they had managed to maintain could shatter completely.

As she entered the lounge, the others were gathered around the fire, their expressions still drawn with the tension of the previous day. Emma glanced up as Clara entered, her eyes filled with worry, but Clara forced a smile, masking the suspicions that were now firmly rooted in her mind.

"Did you manage to get some rest?" Sarah asked, her tone neutral but laced with the same weariness they all felt.

"A little," Clara replied, her voice steady. "I just needed a moment to clear my head."

Daniel was stirring the fire, the flames dancing higher as he added another log. "We all do," he muttered, his gaze fixed on the flames. "It's hard to think straight with everything that's happened."

Clara nodded, taking a seat near the fire but keeping a careful distance from the others. She watched them closely, noting the small tells in their body language, the subtle shifts in their expressions. Emma's nervous fidgeting, Sarah's guarded tone, Daniel's distraction—they were all on edge, all hiding something, even if they didn't realize it.

Margaret, who had been silent since Clara's return, finally spoke up. "What do we do now? We're all running on fumes, and I don't know how much longer we can keep this up."

Clara turned her attention to Margaret, her mind racing as she considered how best to approach the situation. "We need to stay calm," she said, her tone measured. "We've made it this far, and we can't afford to fall apart now. But we also need to start thinking ahead. We're low on supplies, and the storm doesn't seem to be letting up anytime soon."

Sarah looked at Clara, her expression unreadable. "What do you suggest?"

Clara hesitated, choosing her words carefully. "We should ration our food more strictly, maybe even set up a schedule for who's on watch and when. And we need to keep an eye on each other. After everything that's happened… trust is a luxury we can't afford right now."

The others nodded in agreement, though Clara could see the uncertainty in their eyes. They were all struggling with the same doubts, the same fears, but no one wanted to be the first to voice them. That was fine with Clara—it would make it easier for her to observe, to gather the information she needed without raising suspicion.

The morning passed slowly, the atmosphere in the inn heavy with the unspoken tensions that now defined their interactions. Clara watched as the others went about their tasks, each of them trying to maintain some semblance of normalcy in a situation that had long since ceased to be anything but abnormal.

Emma's nervous energy seemed to have intensified, her movements quick and erratic as she moved about the lounge, tidying up and checking the fire. Clara noticed how Emma's hands trembled slightly whenever she reached for something, how her eyes darted around the room as if she were expecting something to happen at any moment.

Sarah and Daniel seemed to be keeping their distance from each other, their interactions brief and tense. Clara couldn't help but wonder if they, too, were starting to suspect one another. The memory of finding them in Alex's room kept gnawing at her, a puzzle piece she couldn't yet fit into place.

Margaret was quiet, her usual warmth and kindness subdued as she went about her tasks. Clara watched her carefully, noting the way Margaret avoided looking at the spot where Charles had been killed. The grief and guilt were evident in Margaret's every movement, but Clara couldn't help but wonder if there was something more beneath the surface— something that Margaret wasn't telling them.

As the day wore on, Clara's resolve only deepened. She couldn't trust any of them—not fully. But she could observe, listen, and wait for the moment when the truth would reveal itself. And when it did, she would be ready.

For now, though, Clara would play her part, pretending to be just as confused and fearful as the rest of them. She would keep her suspicions to herself, bide her time, and gather the pieces of the puzzle until they formed a clear picture.

The others might be hiding secrets, but Clara had her own secrets now. And she intended to keep them until the time was right.

21

Chapter 21

Nightfall brought with it an uneasy quiet that settled over the inn like a thick, suffocating blanket. The fire crackled softly in the hearth, casting flickering shadows across the walls, but the warmth it provided did little to dispel the chill that had settled in Clara's bones. She had managed to convince the others that she needed sleep, but in truth, Clara's mind was far too restless for any real rest. She lay in her bed, fully clothed, with her back to the door and her eyes closed, feigning sleep while keeping her senses on high alert.

Emma and Daniel had taken the first watch, their low voices barely audible from the lounge. Clara strained to catch snippets of their conversation, hoping for something—anything—that might give her more insight into the growing web of mystery and distrust that had engulfed them all. But for the most part, their talk was inconsequential, filled with idle chit-chat and the kind of surface-level exchanges that came when people were too afraid to delve deeper.

Clara shifted slightly, careful not to make any noise that

might give away her wakefulness. She focused on the cadence of their voices, waiting for something, anything, that might provide a clue. For a long time, there was nothing, just the crackling of the fire and the soft murmur of their voices blending into the background.

Then, as if sensing her growing impatience, Daniel said something that made Clara's heart skip a beat.

"It's strange, you know," Daniel began, his voice tinged with a faint unease that Clara hadn't heard before. "Sarah and I were given this trip to the inn as a Christmas present. We didn't even know who sent it—a 'relative' was all the note said. It was odd, but… we figured, why not? A free vacation, right?"

Clara's pulse quickened. A Christmas present from an anonymous relative? That was more than just odd—it was suspicious, especially given everything that had happened since their arrival. Who would send them to this isolated inn, and why? The thought gnawed at Clara, adding another layer of uncertainty to the growing pile of questions in her mind.

Emma's voice was cautious as she replied, "That is strange. I mean, it's not like you and Sarah are hard up for cash. Why wouldn't the relative just tell you who they were?"

Daniel sighed, the sound heavy with the weight of his thoughts. "Exactly. But we didn't think much of it at the time. Maybe we should have."

Clara kept her breathing slow and even, trying to process this new information without betraying her growing suspicion. She was at the inn because she had lost her job, and when she'd gotten home, she'd found a pamphlet for the inn in her mailbox. It had seemed like a sign—a chance to get away, to clear her head, to start fresh. But now, in light of what Daniel had said, Clara couldn't shake the feeling that her presence here was more than just a coincidence.

Who had really sent her the pamphlet? Had it been random, or was there something more deliberate behind it? The questions buzzed in her mind like a swarm of angry bees, but she forced herself to stay calm, to keep listening.

Emma seemed to mull over Daniel's words for a moment before excusing herself. "I'm just going to use the bathroom. I'll be right back."

Daniel murmured an acknowledgment, and the sound of Emma's footsteps faded as she walked away. Clara waited, keeping her breathing steady, her senses alert. But as the minutes ticked by, something began to feel wrong. Too much time had passed, and Emma hadn't returned.

Clara opened her eyes, glancing toward the door. It was still slightly ajar, allowing a sliver of light from the lounge to filter into the room. She listened intently, but all she could hear was the faint crackling of the fire and the ticking of the old clock on the mantelpiece.

Unease coiled in Clara's stomach. She knew she should stay put, but the silence was growing unbearable, and the longer Emma was gone, the more certain Clara became that something was very, very wrong.

Finally, Clara couldn't take it anymore. She swung her legs over the side of the bed and slipped her feet into her shoes. Moving as quietly as she could, she made her way to the door and pushed it open, peering into the hallway.

The inn was eerily quiet, the only light coming from the flickering flames in the lounge. Daniel was still sitting near the fire, his back to her, seemingly lost in thought. But there was no sign of Emma.

Clara took a deep breath and stepped into the hallway, making her way toward the lounge. As she approached, Daniel must have heard her, because he turned around, his expression one of confusion.

"Clara? I thought you were asleep," he said, his voice a little too loud in the stillness of the inn.

Clara ignored the question, her concern for Emma overriding any need for pretense. "Where's Emma? She should have been back by now."

Daniel's brow furrowed, and he glanced toward the hallway that led to the bathrooms. "She said she was going to the bathroom… but that was a while ago, wasn't it?"

A knot of dread tightened in Clara's chest. "We need to find her."

They moved quickly, waking Sarah and Margaret as they passed their rooms. The group gathered near the bathrooms, calling out Emma's name, but there was no response. Clara's unease deepened as they checked the stalls and found them empty. It was as if Emma had simply vanished.

Then, in the midst of their frantic search, Clara noticed something that made her blood run cold. One of the side doors—a door that led outside—was wide open, the cold night air seeping into the hallway.

"Over here!" Clara called, her voice shaking slightly as she pointed to the open door.

The group hurried over, their expressions shifting from concern to outright fear. The door, which had been securely locked earlier in the evening, was now ajar, the darkness outside pressing in like an unwelcome guest.

"Why would she go outside?" Sarah asked, her voice barely above a whisper.

Clara didn't have an answer. The open door was a mystery, and the longer they stood there, the more the tension in the air thickened. There was no sign of Emma, no footprints in the snow leading away from the inn—just the cold, dark night and the gnawing fear that something terrible had happened.

Margaret's voice trembled as she spoke. "We need to look for her. She could be out there… she could be in trouble."

Daniel nodded, his jaw set with determination. "I'll go. Maybe she's just out there, confused or disoriented. We can't leave her out there alone."

Clara felt a surge of anxiety at the thought of Daniel going out alone, but before she could voice her concern, Daniel was already moving, grabbing his coat and a flashlight.

"Be careful," Clara said, her voice tight with worry. "If you find her, bring her back immediately."

Daniel gave a curt nod before stepping out into the night, the beam of his flashlight cutting through the darkness. The cold air rushed in as he closed the door behind him, leaving the remaining three in a tense, uneasy silence.

Clara felt her pulse quicken as she stood there, staring at the door through which both Emma and Daniel had now disappeared. She didn't like this—didn't like the idea of them being out there, alone, in the dark. But what choice did they have? They couldn't just leave Emma out there, and someone had to go after her.

The three women returned to the lounge, their nerves frayed and their thoughts scattered. The fire still burned low in the hearth, casting long shadows on the walls. But as they entered the room, a new sight stopped them in their tracks.

Near the fire, lying on the worn rug, were two dead rabbits. The rabbits were fresh, their fur still soft and clean, their bodies intact but clearly lifeless. The sight was jarring, out of place in the cozy warmth of the lounge, and it sent a chill down Clara's spine.

"What… what is this?" Sarah asked, her voice trembling with fear and confusion.

Margaret's eyes were wide, her hands trembling as she stared at the rabbits. "Is this… some kind of warning? Or… is someone trying to help us?"

Clara approached the rabbits cautiously, her mind racing. The placement of the rabbits was deliberate, that much was clear. But whether it was meant as a threat or a gesture of goodwill was impossible to say. The rabbits could be food—an offering from someone who knew how desperate their situation had become—or they could be a sinister message, a reminder of the ever-present danger that surrounded them.

"We need to be careful," Clara said, her voice steady despite the fear that gnawed at her. "We don't know who left these here, or why. But we should assume that whoever did it was inside the inn at some point tonight."

Margaret looked around the room, her fear palpable. "But that means… that means someone could have been watching us, could still be watching us."

The realization sent a shiver down Clara's spine. The idea that someone could have been lurking in the shadows, watching their every move, filled her with dread. But she couldn't afford to let fear paralyze her—not when they were still in the midst of such a dangerous situation.

"We need to stay together," Clara said firmly. "Until Daniel gets back, we don't split up for any reason. We'll wait here and keep the fire going."

The three women huddled near the fire, their eyes flicking

nervously between the rabbits and the door, waiting for any sign of Daniel's return. The minutes stretched into what felt like hours, the silence thick and oppressive. The warmth of the fire did little to dispel the cold that had settled in Clara's chest, a cold born of fear and uncertainty.

As the night dragged on, Clara's thoughts turned once again to the events that had brought them to this point. The mysterious invitation that had led Sarah and Daniel to the inn, the pamphlet that had lured her here, the strange behavior of the others—it all pointed to something deeper, something they had yet to uncover.

But before Clara could delve further into her thoughts, the silence was shattered by the sound of the side door creaking open.

The three women jumped to their feet, their hearts racing as they stared at the door, waiting for Daniel to return, perhaps with Emma in tow. But as the seconds ticked by and no one appeared, Clara's fear turned to dread.

"Daniel?" Clara called out, her voice trembling slightly.

There was no answer.

Clara exchanged a fearful glance with Sarah and Margaret before slowly moving toward the door. Her hand shook as she reached for the handle, pulling the door open to reveal the dark, snow-covered landscape beyond.

But there was no sign of Daniel. No footprints, no sound, nothing but the cold, silent night.

Clara's heart sank as she realized the terrible truth: Daniel, like Emma, was gone.

Panic threatened to overtake her, but Clara forced herself to remain calm. She couldn't afford to lose control now—not when they were on the brink of losing everything.

"We have to stay calm," Clara said, her voice firm despite the fear that gripped her. "We can't panic. We need to think this through."

Sarah's voice was shaky as she spoke. "What… what do we do? Do we go after them?"

Clara shook her head. "No. We can't risk losing anyone else. We stay here, we wait. If they're out there, they might come back. But we have to be ready for anything."

Margaret nodded, though her face was pale with fear. "You're right. We can't split up again. We have to stay together."

The three women retreated to the lounge, the fire crackling softly in the hearth as they tried to keep their fear at bay. But the sense of dread lingered, a heavy weight that pressed down on them as they waited for the morning light, for some sign of what had happened to Emma and Daniel.

Clara's mind raced as she considered the events of the night, the mysterious disappearance of two of their own, the strange offering of the rabbits. Nothing made sense, and the more she thought about it, the more she realized just how little they truly understood about the danger they were in.

But one thing was certain: they were not alone. Someone— or something—was watching them, playing with them, manipulating them. And until they uncovered the truth, they would remain at the mercy of whatever sinister force had brought them to this point.

As the first light of dawn began to filter through the windows, Clara's resolve hardened. She would find out the truth, no matter what it took. But for now, all they could do was wait— and hope that they weren't the next to disappear into the night.

22

Chapter 22

The morning sun filtered through the windows of the inn, casting a warm glow that belied the tension lingering in the air. The events of the previous night weighed heavily on Clara, Sarah, and Margaret as they gathered in the kitchen, their nerves frayed and their thoughts scattered. Daniel and Emma were still missing, and the mystery of their disappearance hung over them like a dark cloud.

Margaret stood at the counter, her hands working with practiced ease as she prepared to clean the rabbits they had found near the fire the night before. Her movements were methodical, almost mechanical, as if she were trying to distract herself from the fear gnawing at the edges of her mind.

Sarah joined her, a knife in hand, as she began chopping a few spare vegetables they had managed to scrounge up from the pantry. The rhythmic sound of the knife against the cutting board was oddly soothing, filling the otherwise silent kitchen with a steady, familiar rhythm.

Clara watched them work, her mind still racing with questions she couldn't yet answer. As she observed Sarah's precise knife skills, a thought occurred to her, and she decided to voice it.

"You're really good with that knife, Sarah," Clara said casually, though her eyes were sharp as she watched Sarah's reaction. "Where'd you learn how to chop like that?"

Sarah didn't look up from her task, her focus seemingly on the vegetables she was dicing. "I went to culinary school," she replied, her tone neutral. "I didn't finish, but I learned enough to be decent in the kitchen."

Clara nodded, though her thoughts were now tinged with suspicion. Culinary school would certainly explain Sarah's skill with a knife, but it also made Clara wonder just how much more Sarah might be capable of. She knew from experience that knife skills weren't just for the kitchen—they could be used for much darker purposes as well.

Margaret, who had been quiet for most of the morning, suddenly looked up from her work. "The rabbits will make a good stew," she said, her voice steady despite the tremor in her hands. "We should eat something warm, keep our strength up."

Clara seized the opportunity to steer the conversation in a new direction. "Margaret, do you have any hunting rifles here at the inn? Just in case… you know, we need them."

Margaret's expression clouded over, and she shook her head. "No, I don't. My husband used to have a couple, but they're gone now. He… he died a few years ago, and I didn't keep them. I never liked hunting. I'm more of a homemaker."

The sadness in Margaret's voice was palpable, and Clara felt a pang of guilt for bringing up a painful memory. But she couldn't afford to let sentiment cloud her judgment. There were too many unanswered questions, and she needed to start piecing together the truth.

"What does Daniel do for a living?" Clara asked, her tone as casual as she could manage. She watched Sarah carefully, noting the subtle tension that seemed to creep into her posture.

"He's a plastic surgeon," Sarah replied, her voice betraying nothing. "He's very good at what he does."

Clara's mind raced. A plastic surgeon and a chef with knife skills—both professions required a steady hand, precision, and an intimate knowledge of anatomy. The realization sent a chill down Clara's spine. Both Sarah and Daniel had the skills necessary to carry out the brutal slashing of the captives' throats. The pieces of the puzzle were starting to fit together, but the picture they formed was one that Clara wasn't sure she wanted to see.

The three women worked in silence for a few more minutes, the tension in the room thickening with each passing second. Clara's mind was racing, trying to make sense of everything she had learned. Finally, she decided to shift the conversation again, hoping to glean more information.

"This inn really is something special," Clara said, her voice carefully measured. "So cozy and peaceful. It's easy to see why people would want to come here."

Margaret smiled, though it didn't reach her eyes. "Yes, it is. My husband and I poured our hearts into this place. It was our dream to create a little sanctuary where people could escape from the world for a while."

Sarah, who had been quiet, suddenly spoke up. "That's why Daniel and I decided to come here. It was a gift from my uncle—a vacation to get away from it all. We thought it would be a nice change of pace."

Clara's ears perked up at Sarah's words. "Your uncle?" she asked, feigning casual curiosity. "Daniel mentioned last night that the trip was a gift from an anonymous relative. But you said it was your uncle?"

Sarah's hands stilled, and a flicker of panic crossed her face. It was brief, but Clara caught it. "Yes," Sarah replied, her voice a little too quick. "I mean, we didn't know it was from him at first. The note was vague, but later he called to confirm it was him."

Clara's suspicion deepened. Something wasn't adding up. She had caught Sarah in a lie, and now she needed to press further, to see how far Sarah would go to cover her tracks.

"Why didn't Daniel mention that your uncle confirmed it?" Clara asked, her voice laced with just enough doubt to unsettle Sarah further. "It seems like something he would have remembered."

Sarah's eyes darted around the room, her panic more evident now. "I… I don't know. Maybe he forgot. Or maybe he didn't think it was important."

Clara took a step closer, her gaze locked on Sarah's. "Or maybe there's more to the story than you're letting on. Why are you really here, Sarah?"

The question hung in the air, the weight of it pressing down on the room like a lead blanket. Sarah's face paled, and she took a small step back, her hand tightening around the knife she was holding.

"I… I don't…" Sarah stammered, her eyes wide with fear.

Before Clara could press further, Sarah's fear turned into something darker—desperation. In a sudden, frantic movement, Sarah lunged forward and plunged the knife into Margaret's stomach.

Margaret gasped, her eyes wide with shock and pain as she clutched her stomach, blood seeping through her fingers. Clara's heart raced as she watched Margaret collapse to the floor, the life draining from her eyes.

"No!" Clara screamed, rushing toward Margaret, but Sarah was already on the move. Without a second thought, Sarah bolted from the kitchen, the knife still in her hand.

Clara's mind whirled with panic and anger, but she couldn't let Sarah get away. She had to stop her, had to find out the truth. Ignoring the searing pain of her emotions, Clara dashed after Sarah, her feet pounding against the wooden floorboards as she raced through the inn.

Sarah headed for the shed, the one place outside the inn where she might be able to hide or make her escape. Clara followed close behind, her breath coming in ragged gasps as she pushed herself to catch up.

The shed loomed ahead, its door slightly ajar, and Clara knew she couldn't let Sarah disappear into the night. With a burst of adrenaline, Clara lunged forward, grabbing Sarah by the arm just as she reached the door.

The two women struggled, their bodies slamming into the side of the shed as they grappled for control. Sarah slashed wildly with the knife, but Clara managed to deflect the blows, using every ounce of strength she had left.

"Why did you do it, Sarah?" Clara demanded, her voice raw with emotion. "Why?"

Sarah's face twisted with a mix of fear and anger. "I didn't have a choice! You don't understand!"

"Then help me understand!" Clara shouted, her grip tightening as she tried to wrestle the knife from Sarah's hand.

The two women continued to struggle, but Clara's determination gave her the edge. With one final push, she knocked Sarah to the ground, the knife clattering to the floor of the shed. Clara pounced, pinning Sarah down and knocking her out with a sharp blow to the temple.

Panting heavily, Clara finally let herself collapse to the ground beside Sarah, her body trembling with exhaustion and fear. But the sound of a low groan caught her attention, and Clara turned her head toward the corner of the shed.

Her heart dropped when she saw Emma's nearly lifeless body lying in the shadows, her face pale and her eyes staring blankly at Clara. Blood pooled around her, her throat slashed, but not as deep as the captives. Clara felt a sob rise in her throat, but there was no time to break down—there was still too much at stake.

Just as Clara was about to get to her feet, she felt a sharp, searing pain in her side. She looked down to see the blade of a knife protruding from her abdomen—Daniel's knife. He had crept up on her in the chaos, and now he was plunging the blade into her flesh again and again, his face contorted with rage and desperation.

Clara's vision blurred, pain shooting through her body as she fought to stay conscious. She struggled against Daniel, her strength waning with each passing second, but she refused to give up. Summoning every ounce of willpower she had left, Clara twisted her body and managed to knock the knife from Daniel's hand.

But before she could escape, Daniel grabbed her by the throat, his grip tightening as he forced her to the ground. Clara gasped for breath, her vision darkening as she fought to break free. She knew she was losing the fight, that her strength was fading fast.

But just as the darkness threatened to take her, a gunshot rang out, echoing through the shed like a clap of thunder. Daniel's grip on her throat loosened, and he collapsed to the ground, blood pouring from a wound in his chest.

Clara coughed, sucking in a ragged breath as she looked up to see Margaret standing in the doorway of the shed, a hunting rifle clutched in her trembling hands. Margaret's face was ashen, blood still seeping from the wound in her stomach, but she had managed to make her way to the shed, determined to save Clara.

"Margaret…" Clara rasped, her voice weak.

Margaret stumbled forward, her strength fading fast. She dropped to her knees beside Clara, her breath coming in shallow gasps. "I… I couldn't let him kill you," Margaret whispered, tears filling her eyes.

Clara reached out, gripping Margaret's hand with the last of her strength. "Thank you," she whispered, her vision blurring once more as unconsciousness loomed.

The two women lay there in the shed, surrounded by the carnage and chaos that had consumed their lives. The fight was over, but the cost had been devastating. As Clara's vision faded to black, she couldn't help but wonder if they would ever find the answers they had been searching for, or if the darkness that had claimed so many would finally claim them too.

23

Chapter 23

The cold air bit at Clara's exposed skin as she stumbled through the snow-covered woods, each step a painful reminder of the injuries she had sustained. Blood seeped through her clothes, staining the white snow with dark patches that marked her path. She was disoriented, her vision blurred and her mind clouded with a mix of fear and determination. She had to find help—had to escape before it was too late.

Clara's breath came in ragged gasps, her body growing weaker with each passing moment. She had no idea how long she had been walking, but the thick forest seemed endless, the trees stretching on in every direction. Her thoughts were a jumble of memories and questions, none of them making any sense. All she knew was that she had to keep moving, had to find a way out of this nightmare.

Suddenly, through the trees, Clara spotted something— an outline against the stark white of the snow. As she got closer, her heart leaped with a flicker of hope. It was Charles's snowmobile, half-buried in a drift but still intact. The sight of it gave her a surge of energy she didn't know she had left.

Staggering toward the snowmobile, Clara almost collapsed as she reached it. With trembling hands, she brushed the snow off the seat and climbed on, wincing in pain as she did. Her fingers were numb, making it difficult to turn the key, but after a few desperate tries, the engine roared to life.

The snowmobile lurched forward, nearly throwing her off, but Clara held on with all the strength she had left. The wind whipped around her, the cold biting into her exposed skin, but she didn't care. She just needed to reach the road, to find someone who could help.

The snowmobile plowed through the snow, the trees blurring past her as she sped through the forest. Clara's vision was fading, her consciousness slipping away with every jolt and bump. But she couldn't stop—not yet. She had to keep going, had to escape.

Finally, after what felt like an eternity, Clara saw a break in the trees ahead—a road. Relief flooded through her as she steered the snowmobile onto the pavement, the smooth surface offering a momentary respite from the relentless jolts of the forest trail.

But her relief was short-lived. The world around her began to spin, her vision darkening at the edges. The last thing Clara saw before everything went black was the blurred outline of a car approaching from the distance.

Clara awoke in a stark, white room, the sterile smell of antiseptic filling her nostrils. The bright lights above her head were blinding, making her squint as she tried to make sense of her surroundings. Her body felt heavy, her limbs unresponsive, and as she tried to move, she realized with a jolt of fear that she was strapped to the bed.

Panic set in as Clara struggled against the restraints, her heart pounding in her chest. "Where am I?" she croaked, her voice hoarse and weak. "What's happening?"

A man in a white coat appeared at the foot of her bed, his expression calm and clinical. "Good morning, Clara," he said in a soothing voice that only made her more anxious. "You're in a hospital. You were found unconscious on the side of the road."

Clara's mind raced as she tried to piece together what had happened. The last thing she remembered was the snowmobile, the road… and then nothing. But now she was here, in a hospital, strapped to a bed. Something wasn't right.

"Why am I tied down?" Clara demanded, her voice trembling with fear. "What's going on?"

The doctor's expression remained neutral, his tone professional. "Clara, you've been placed in a psychiatric facility for your own safety. When you were found, you were in a highly agitated state, and we had to ensure that you wouldn't harm yourself or others."

Clara's heart sank as his words registered. A psychiatric facility? This had to be some kind of mistake. "No, no, you don't understand," she protested, her voice growing more frantic. "There was an attack at the inn. Margaret can explain everything. She was with me—she saved me!"

The doctor's eyes softened with what Clara could only describe as pity. "Clara, Margaret's body was found in the attic of the inn. According to the autopsy, she had been dead for at least a month."

Clara's breath caught in her throat, her mind reeling with confusion and horror. "No," she whispered, shaking her head in denial. "That's not possible. I was with her. She was alive… She… I…"

The doctor reached into his pocket and pulled out a photograph, holding it up for Clara to see. The image showed the lifeless body of an older woman, her features gaunt and decayed from weeks of death. But it wasn't the Margaret that Clara had known—it was a stranger.

"That's not her," Clara insisted, her voice growing more desperate. "That's not the Margaret I knew. This is a mistake!"

The doctor's expression remained unreadable as he tucked the photograph away. "Clara, we have witnesses and evidence that contradict your version of events. The housekeeper, who survived, stated that you went mad and killed everyone at the inn, including two FBI agents who were posing as vacationers."

Clara felt as though the ground had been ripped out from under her. FBI agents? Daniel and Sarah were FBI agents? None of it made sense. "No, no, that's not true!" Clara cried, tears streaming down her face. "I didn't kill anyone! I swear! There was someone else… they were the ones who did it!"

But the doctor only shook his head, his voice calm but firm. "Clara, I know this is difficult for you to understand right now, but you need to accept the reality of the situation. You've been through a traumatic experience, and your mind is trying to make sense of it in ways that aren't based on reality."

Clara's protests fell on deaf ears as the doctor turned and walked toward the door. "I'll leave you to rest," he said over his shoulder. "The nurse will be in shortly to give you your medication."

As the doctor left the room, Clara could hear him speaking to someone outside the door, though she couldn't make out the words. Her mind raced, a whirlwind of confusion, fear, and disbelief. How had everything gone so wrong? How had she ended up here, blamed for murders she didn't commit?

The door opened again, and a nurse entered, a small cup of pills in one hand and a glass of water in the other. "Time for your meds," the nurse said kindly, though her eyes held a hint of caution as she approached the bed.

Clara stared at the pills, her mind screaming at her to refuse, to fight, to do something. But she was weak, her body battered and her spirit broken. Reluctantly, she opened her mouth and swallowed the pills, feeling the cold water wash them down her throat.

The nurse gave her a small, reassuring smile before leaving the room, the door clicking shut behind her. Clara lay there in the silence, the drugs already beginning to dull her senses, her thoughts growing hazy and disjointed.

Days passed, each one blending into the next as Clara sank deeper into a fog of medication and despair. She tried to piece together what had happened, but every time she thought she was close to understanding, the drugs would pull her back into a numbing void.

Then, one day, Clara received a visitor.

Emma.

Clara blinked in surprise, her mind struggling to make sense of what she was seeing. Emma stood at the foot of her bed, her expression calm and composed, as if she hadn't just walked into a psychiatric facility to visit someone accused of murder.

"Emma," Clara croaked, her voice weak from disuse. "You're alive…"

Emma nodded, a small smile playing on her lips. "Yes, I am. And I wanted to thank you, Clara."

Clara frowned, confusion clouding her mind. "Thank me?

For what?"

"For helping us find the treasure," Emma said, her tone light, almost conversational. "My mother and I couldn't have done it without you."

Clara's heart began to race, a sense of dread creeping into her chest. "Emma, what are you talking about? You have to tell them the truth. You have to tell them I didn't kill anyone!"

But Emma's smile only widened, her eyes cold and calculating. "Oh, Clara, you were so helpful. But I'm afraid the truth isn't quite what you think it is."

Clara's breath caught in her throat, her mind racing as she tried to make sense of Emma's words. "What… what do you mean?"

"My mother and I were looking for that treasure for a long time," Emma continued, ignoring Clara's question. "But we needed someone like you to help us get close to it. Someone who was smart, but could be… manipulated."

Clara's world began to crumble as the pieces of the puzzle finally clicked into place. "Margaret is your mother? You… you set me up."

Emma's smile turned cruel. "It was nothing personal, Clara. You were just the right person at the right time. And now that we have what we wanted, there's no need for you anymore. Besides, we get so bored in those winter inns. Sometimes, we like to have fun and play games."

Clara felt a wave of nausea wash over her, the betrayal cutting deeper than any knife ever could. "A game? That's what it was? Just a game? Emma, please… you have to tell them the truth. I didn't do anything wrong."

But Emma's expression remained cold and unyielding. "The truth doesn't matter, Clara. What matters is that my mother and I have the treasure, and you… well, you're just a convenient scapegoat."

Tears filled Clara's eyes as the reality of her situation sank in. She had been used, manipulated, and now she was trapped in a nightmare from which there was no escape.

Emma leaned in closer, her voice soft and mocking. "And if you're ever in the area, do come visit our new inn. The old owner died, so we bought it. It's going to be a real treasure. I hear there is a fortune to be made in real estate."

Clara's heart shattered as Emma turned and walked out of the room, leaving her alone in the sterile, white cell. The door clicked shut behind her, the sound echoing in the emptiness of Clara's soul.

She had lost everything—her freedom, her sanity, her hope. And now she was trapped, blamed for murders she didn't commit, with no one to believe her and no way to prove her innocence.

As the medication began to take hold once more, Clara's thoughts drifted into a foggy haze, her mind retreating into the darkness that had claimed so much of her life.

But even in the depths of her despair, one thought remained, a flicker of defiance that refused to be extinguished.

She would find a way out. She had to.

Even if it was the last thing she ever did.

24

Chapter 24

The wind howled through the trees, sending flurries of snow spiraling through the air as the isolated inn stood, a lone sentinel against the encroaching night. The fresh blanket of snow covered the landscape in a pristine white, untouched by human presence—save for the single set of tracks that led to the front door of the inn. Inside, the warmth of a crackling fire filled the air with a sense of coziness that belied the true nature of the place.

Margaret stood at the front door, her face illuminated by the soft glow of the lantern she held in her hand. The wind whipped her graying hair around her face, but she paid it no mind. She had been waiting for this moment, preparing for it ever since last year.

A faint crunch of snow underfoot announced the arrival of the new guest. Margaret's smile was welcoming, warm, and utterly deceptive as she opened the door wider, allowing the cold to sweep briefly into the inn before the door closed with a soft thud behind her.

"Heather, welcome," Margaret said, her voice smooth and

inviting. "I'm so glad you could make it."

Heather, a woman in her mid-thirties with tired eyes and a worn expression, gave Margaret a tentative smile as she stepped inside, grateful for the warmth that immediately enveloped her. She shrugged off her heavy coat, handing it to Margaret with a murmured thank you.

"It's so cold out there," Heather said, rubbing her hands together as she looked around the inn's cozy interior. "I wasn't sure I'd find the place in this weather."

Margaret's smile widened, a glint of something dark flickering in her eyes. "The snow can be unforgiving up here, but once you're inside, it's like a little slice of heaven. Come, sit by the fire. Two of our guests have already turned in for the night, but Emma is in the lounge, and I'll bring us all some tea to warm up."

Heather nodded gratefully and followed Margaret's gesture toward the lounge. The room was bathed in the soft glow of the fire, the flames casting dancing shadows on the walls. Emma sat in one of the armchairs, her legs curled beneath her as she stared into the fire, her expression serene. She looked up as Heather entered, offering a small smile that didn't quite reach her eyes.

"Hi, you must be Heather," Emma said, her voice pleasant but distant. "Come, sit by the fire. It's the best spot in the house."

Heather took a seat in the armchair opposite Emma, her eyes flicking around the room as she tried to take in her surroundings. There was something about the inn—something she couldn't quite put her finger on—that made her uneasy, but she pushed the feeling aside. She had come here to escape, to find some peace, and she wasn't about to let her nerves get the better of her.

In the kitchen, Margaret moved with practiced ease as she prepared the tea. She selected a delicate china cup for Heather, filling it with steaming liquid before reaching into the pocket of her apron and retrieving a small vial. With a quick, practiced motion, she tipped the contents of the vial into Heather's cup, watching as the powder dissolved instantly in the hot tea.

Satisfied, Margaret placed the cup on a tray along with two others, each filled with tea but unadulterated by the contents of the vial. She picked up the tray and made her way back to the lounge, her footsteps silent on the worn wooden floor.

As she entered the room, Margaret's smile remained fixed, the perfect mask of hospitality. "Here we are, ladies," she said, setting the tray down on the small table between the armchairs. "A nice cup of tea to warm us all up."

Heather reached for her cup, wrapping her hands around the warm porcelain as she took a grateful sip. The tea was strong, slightly bitter, but she paid it no mind. The warmth spread through her, easing the chill that had settled in her bones during the long journey to the inn.

Margaret watched her for a moment, a hint of satisfaction in her eyes, before turning to Emma. "I'll leave you two to get acquainted," she said softly. "I need to check on a few things in the kitchen."

Emma nodded, her gaze drifting back to the fire as she cradled her own cup of tea. Heather sipped slowly, feeling the warmth seep into her limbs, relaxing her in a way she hadn't felt in a long time.

As Margaret left the lounge, she felt a presence close behind her, and a familiar voice whispered in her ear. "The gun has blanks, right?"

Margaret didn't need to turn around to know who was speaking. The voice belonged to Charles, the man who had been at her side for as long as she could remember, the man who had helped orchestrate everything that had come before.

"Yes," Margaret replied in a low voice, her lips barely moving as she spoke. "Everything is as it should be. Have you set up all of the snow machines?"

Charles's chuckle was dark, filled with anticipation. "Yes. Then the game begins again."

Margaret's smile returned, but this time it was filled with something cold and calculating, something that had nothing to do with warmth or hospitality. She continued down the hallway, her thoughts already moving ahead, planning the next steps in the twisted game they had set in motion.

In the lounge, Heather's eyelids grew heavy, her mind growing foggy as the effects of the pills began to take hold. She blinked slowly, trying to shake off the drowsiness that was creeping up on her, but it was no use. Her body felt like lead, and her thoughts became sluggish, disjointed.

Emma watched her carefully, her expression unreadable as she sipped her tea. The fire crackled softly, filling the silence with its steady, comforting rhythm. But there was nothing comforting about the atmosphere in the room—only a growing sense of inevitability, of a game being played with rules that Heather had yet to understand.

As Heather's vision blurred and the world around her began to fade, she barely registered Emma's soft voice, a final warning that fell on deaf ears.

"Welcome to the game, Heather," Emma whispered. "I hope you're ready."

Heather's cup slipped from her fingers, falling to the floor with a soft clink as she slumped back in the chair, unconscious. Emma watched her for a moment longer before setting her own cup down on the table. The fire continued to burn brightly in the hearth, its warmth a stark contrast to the cold, calculated plans that had been set in motion.

Outside, the snow continued to fall, covering the tracks that led to the inn, erasing any evidence of the new guest's arrival. The world outside remained silent, isolated, and unaware of the dark game that had just begun anew within the walls of the inn.

Margaret returned to the lounge, her expression calm as she surveyed the scene before her. Heather was unconscious, Emma was waiting, and Charles was already moving through the shadows, preparing for what came next. Emma waved through the window pain and blew a kiss at Alex, who was waiting for his cue.

Margaret's smile returned, the perfect picture of a gracious hostess. The game had begun again, and this time, they were ready.

The isolated inn stood as it always had, a place of refuge for those seeking escape, unaware that within its walls, escape was the last thing they would find.

And so, the snow fell, the fire burned, and the game went on, as it always had—and as it always would.

The End

9 798227 865328